Wang unloaded most of the weapons from his bag and strapped them on to make carrying them easier. Duel Uzis in holsters over the shoulders, riot gun in a sheath along his left leg, grenade launcher on the right, rail gun across his chest; and shuriken, grenades, sticky bombs, caltrops, and all the other hand-held gadgets he could fit all along the loops on his belt. Night-vision goggles, binoculars, and medkit went into pockets. He tucked ammunition into every spare crevice, but he continued to carry the much-lightened bag.

"You mean there's more in there?" Flo asked incredulously. "What could possibly be left?"

"Oh, just more of same," Wang said casually. He didn't want to worry her needlessly. He was nearly sure he wouldn't need the pocket nuclear bomb, but you never knew.

SHADOW WARRIOR™

YOU ONLY DIE TWICE

Ryan Hughes

POCKET BOOKS

New York London Toronto Sydney Tokyo Singapore

An *Original* Publication of POCKET BOOKS

POCKET BOOKS, a division of Simon & Schuster Inc.
1230 Avenue of the Americas, New York, NY 10020

You Only Die Twice © 1997 Apogee Software, Ltd. All rights
reserved. Published by Pocket Books under license from GT
Interactive Software Corp. Based on the computer game
Shadow Warrior™ © 1997 3D Realms Entertainment, Inc.
All rights reserved.

ISBN: 0-671-01880-9

First Pocket Books printing October 1997

10 9 8 7 6 5 4 3 2 1

POCKET and colophon are registered trademarks of
Simon & Schuster Inc.

Printed in the U.S.A.

*For Dean Wesley Smith
and John Ordover—
Wang Lo, guys.*

YOU ONLY DIE TWICE

Chapter 1

When the cavern roof fell in on him, the biggest surprise for Lo Wang was that his life actually did flash before his eyes as he died. It was also his biggest disappointment, for the badly edited movie, more than anything else, meant he had finally become a Westerner.

While his battered brain reeled through a random moment in his life—the time he had accidentally dismembered a street mime by striking out too quickly when he felt what he thought was a pickpocket's touch on his money belt—Wang fought to regain mental control. A true ninja would spend his last moments preparing his soul for passage into the next life or quietly contemplating the zen of nonexistence or even cursing the gods who had led him to this sorry state, but he would never waste time going over old triumphs and old regrets. That was so western, so American, so—so *whiney*. Even as he realized the metaphysical implications of the thought, Wang regretted very much that he had allowed his karma to sink this low. He would spend a long time on the wheel of existence making up for it.

The boulders piled atop him groaned and settled an inch. When the explosion had brought down the ceiling of the cave he had dived in beside the first coffin-sized block of limestone to fall, hoping it would block the rest from crushing him. It had almost worked, but now he was trapped and bleeding beneath tons of precariously balanced rock. It would only be a matter of time—and not much time at that—before a slide finished the job.

Had Florelle, the woman who had come with him to rescue her mother, survived? Wang called out to her. "Flo? Can you hear me, Flo?" His voice echoed among the rocks, but whether it penetrated far, or whether she was alive to respond even if it did, he didn't know. He heard no sounds other than the creak of boulders that hadn't settled yet. Wang felt vibrations against his back, but he didn't know if they were generated locally by the rockfall or if he was feeling ripples from the earthquakes that raged all around the planet.

Poor Flo. She'd gotten in way over her head. Her poor mother, too. Dr. K.D. Morgan, "Katie" to her scientist friends, had been kidnapped by Exo and forced to use her research device in his evil plan to reshape the world. Flo had joined Wang in his attempt to rescue her, but he had failed them both.

Another moment came unbidden to him, a moment from much earlier in his life, when he had come across a group of thugs tormenting a fat old woman who had dropped a basket full of fish in the market-place. Wang had stooped down, picked up a scaly silver fish in each hand, and as he stood up he had flung them like glittering knives straight into the eyes of two of the attackers. The one who survived still wore an eyepatch over the shattered socket, and considered himself lucky to have survived Wang's *quon gur,* or holy mackerel technique. None of the others had ever tormented an old woman again. That incident had helped Wang's karma, but it was so long ago, he doubted if it counterbalanced more than one or two days of mundane existence in America.

There must have been half a mountain resting on his chest. He was glad he wasn't a big man; even for someone only five foot seven and one hundred seventy-five pounds, there was barely room to breathe in the tiny crevice. He was also glad he wore no shirt. The extra thickness of cloth would have deprived him of precious molecules of air. His tight black leggings and weapons belt were restrictive enough the way they caught the rough limestone and prevented him from sliding forward.

His right arm was held beneath him, but with his left hand he explored the ragged edges of rock that pinned him down. He was careful not to push or pull on anything. The cold, rough boulders were precari-ously stacked; the slightest force could shift them and bring them crashing down the rest of the way.

Wang considered doing just that. The rocks held him in a grainy grip that not even he could break. The fact that he had lodged in a crevice between boulders and hadn't been crushed to a bloody slick was little comfort; at least that would have rung down the

3

curtain on his last act and allowed him to join the choir invisible with a shred of dignity.

He had certainly earned it. He was rather proud of that last fight. Trapped in a cavern with mutated tiger-men and snake-men and even a rabid feral-pig-man, he had adopted each one's unique fighting style and used their own tricks against them. The rocky floor with which he was now intimately familiar was slick with their blood. He had fought like a ninja. No, better than a ninja; he had fought like a Shadow Warrior. Shadow Warriors were the best of the best, and it was not arrogance to admit that he, Lo Wang, was the best of the Shadow Warriors.

But even the best can still lose a battle, and Wang had lost this one. Dr. Exo, the mastermind behind the global catastrophe that continued overhead even now, had lured him into this cavern and set his mutated minions on him, and while Wang had overcome them, he hadn't been quick enough to stop Exo from detonating the remote-control bomb that had brought down the ceiling. Now Exo could continue his mad plan to reunite all the continents of the world into Pangaea, and not long after Wang's own death, the world as humanity knew it would come to an end.

Jefferson Adams would keep trying to stop him, of course, but Wang had witnessed his methods. Exo had nothing to fear from him. Only another Shadow Warrior could defeat Exo, and even that seemed unlikely, given Wang's own failure.

The best of the best. Who would inherit his title when his heart pumped its final beat? The thought brought a whole cascade of images into his head. One in particular locked into place.

Shoji, his first instructor, the few wispy gray hairs on the top of his head sticking comically into the air the way they always did when he exerted himself. "Quickly, little one," the old man said, straightening up after snapping the top few inches off a wrist-thick wooden pole with only two fingers of his left hand. The splintered end wobbled slightly, but the pole, balanced only on its flat bottom, did not tip over. "You must move quickly. Remember that kinetic energy is equal to one half mass times velocity squared. *Squared.*" He smiled as if imparting great wisdom rather than the gibberish he was spouting. For this Wang paid eight thousand yen a week? His disdain must have shown, for Shoji suddenly lost his smile and shouted, "Baka! This is a fundamental truth of the universe! Great minds worked for centuries to understand it, the life of every creature that breathes depends on it—the planets themselves hang in its delicate balance—and it is not for you, a simple child of no breeding and even less talent, to roll your eyes as though I have wasted your precious time when I speak it aloud! Your ears are not fit to receive such holy truth, but I will repeat it for you one more time: Kinetic energy is equal to one half mass times velocity squared."

The young Lo Wang dutifully committed the nonsense words to memory. "But—but—what does it mean?" he asked, proud at least that his voice did not quiver beneath his master's rage.

"I told you, it means move quickly. Carry nothing extra in your hand to increase its bulk, for that slows down your attack. Keep it light and strike quickly, for speed counts far more than mass." Master Shoji wiped a drop of perspiration from his forehead and dabbed it on his white robe. On the way from head to cloth his hand deviated slightly from a straight path, just a momentary blur, but there was a sharp crack and another few inches of wooden pole tumbled end over end to the floor.

"Kay equals one half em vee squared. Now you try it," said Shoji.

Wang had immediately struck at the post with his flattened hand, sure he would draw back only broken fingers, but just as his skin touched wood he felt something brush past beneath his palm and another section of post toppled to the floor.

"A butterfly beat you to it," said Shoji. "Again."

Wang struck once more, bending down to reach the much shortened pole, and this time he felt sharp fire lance up his arm. The pole bounced noisily across the floor, still intact. He pulled back, rubbing his hand. It wasn't broken.

"You are lucky I nudged it with my toe," said Shoji. "You must be faster. Faster than the wind, faster than thought, perhaps faster even than light itself."

Embarrassed, but equally impressed, Wang bowed and said, "I will learn to be faster than light, sensei."

"Wrong!" Shoji cackled. "That is impossible. The tau factor—the square root of the quantity one minus your velocity squared divided by the speed of light squared—forbids it. But you can easily be faster than thought if you use your own brain as the standard."

Wang had not killed him for that insult, not even later when he had acquired sufficient skill. Shoji was the master, after all, and Wang's doorway into the mysteries of *kara te*. Wang had instead learned all he could learn from the aged instructor, right up until the time a year and a half later when Shoji had tripped on the hem of his hakama and cracked his head against the stone pathway in the garden just outside the dojo.

By then Wang had learned enough to tell, just from his master's breathing, that the wound was fatal. He had bent down to receive the learned man's dying words, but Shoji had only said, "Remember, the coefficient of friction is dependent upon two things: the nature of the surface and . . ." before passing on to an alternate plane of existence.

Wang had studied long and hard before he had learned the rest of that universal law, and he had never forgotten it. He had also taken to wearing tighter clothing.

Yes, Master Shoji would have been a good candidate for the title of Shadow Warrior, had he lived.

Something touched Wang's leg, there in the darkness beneath the mountain. Something warm and wet. "Wait your turn, worms," he grunted, tensing his muscles and slamming his leg sideways to crush whatever it was, but the slippery splash told him it was merely blood, still flowing from the corpses of his enemies. He could smell it, too, still warm and metallic in the stuffy cavern air. Along with that came the dry, almost gunpowdery smell of fractured rock and the filthy, fetid stench of unwashed beast bodies.

Enemies. So many enemies. Could one of the ones he had not killed today be about to receive Wang's title? No single man had ever been as good as Wang, but someone had to be second best, and when the current master died they would inherit the pinnacle by default. Since he had gone independent, Wang had far more enemies than friends, so the odds were great that his successor was indeed someone whom he would have eventually faced in battle had things gone otherwise here.

The thought didn't bother him. Fate governed a ninja's life, fate and the leaders of Japan's great commercial and familial empires. Who you worked for was a matter of chance more than anything else, for nobody could know the true nature of his employer until long after he had committed his life to their service. Often when empires clashed, ninja who had trained together, even fought together at other times, wound up fighting one another. That was karma. Nobody took it personally. Most enemies weren't evil; they were merely enemies.

So which one would be the most powerful Shadow Warrior a few minutes hence? When you reach the top of your profession, you know all the others within reach. Wang ran down the list of possibilities. There was Iyé Kinjiru, the silent, forbidding boy who had studied with him under Master Shoji and who had later earned a reputation for assassinating impossible-to-reach targets by killing their underlings one at a time until the survivors banded together and killed the man he wanted so Kinjiru would spare their lives. Or Gomen Nasai, the humble, apologetic man who always told his victims exactly what it was that fate was about to force him to do to them, and then did it without deviation from his plan even when they used that knowledge to defend themselves. Both of them had what so many others lacked: *style.*

But style alone did not mean they were the best. Kara Anata fought with all the uniqueness of a rice grain, but he obeyed all the forms and he never made a mistake. A person could go a long way in life simply by not making any mistakes.

All the way to the top? No. That required creativity as well. Creativity and a forum to show off your talents. It didn't do any good to be the best assassin in the business if nobody knew you were *in* the business. You needed to be part of an organization.

Somewhere in the dark a rock screeched as it shifted under the weight of all those above it. The effect rippled through the collapsed cavern, and the boulder pressing into Wang's chest dropped another half inch. Now he could breathe only in tiny gasps. A sharp edge of limestone pressed into his ear, and when he tried to move his head he realized that was trapped now, too. The rock sliced into his earlobe; a trickle of blood started down his neck from the fresh wound.

In the moment of distraction, his oxygen-deprived brain flashed another scene before him: the day he had gone to work for Zilla Enterprises. He hadn't known he would become gainfully employed that day—he still had plenty of money from the last independent job he had done—but fate had intervened in a crowded restaurant and forever changed his life.

Chapter 2

The place was called Hi Fat's Wokkery Cookery. It was new, and Wang had heard good things about it, so he had come to check it out. So far he was unimpressed. The food smelled wonderful—teriyaki and fresh fish and roasted pheasant predominated—but the place was crowded and noisy and hot. It was hard to hear over the conversation and the fusion Taiko drumming-rap music coming from speakers hung in all four corners, plus Wang had to wait at the counter while the chef made a big show of stir-frying his lunch, hoping for a big tip. He was considering whether a knife at the chef's neck would speed him up or merely distract him when two men entered the restaurant and everything stopped.

The dozens of conversations that had been going on all around him, the clatter of chopsticks on bowls, even the show-off chef stopped moving in the same instant. Someone switched off the drum-rap music.

The two men walked to the counter as if nothing unusual had happened. Wang didn't know them, but the local patrons certainly did. One man wore a dark gray business suit that advertised great wealth and the other wore dark blue and carried himself like a cat. Wang recognized that walk; he had seen it many times in the students of another great martial arts instructor. When the man in blue came up beside him, Wang said casually, "Master Nekko?"

He never got a response, for a six-pointed shuriken suddenly buried itself in the man's temple, and he crumpled to the floor at Wang's feet. Wang stepped back and looked in the direction the fighting star had come from, saw a man who had been eating a plate of sashimi throw another at the man in gray.

Irritated that the assassin should kill a man he was trying to speak to, Wang flicked a finger outward to intercept the shuriken, careful to avoid its poisoned points, and deflected it so that it missed the man in gray and stuck in the menu board beside his head. Wang also deflected the six more shuriken that followed. The final one was aimed at him, so Wang caught it by clapping his hands together, then casually flipped it back at the attacker, where it entered neatly between the second and third ribs and severed the man's aorta from his heart. The attacker fell face-first into his sashimi, and his chopsticks clattered to the floor.

"You know that corpse?" Wang asked the man in the gray suit.

"N—no."

Wang noted with amusement that he had to steady himself against the counter.

Wang turned to the cook. "Do not burn my lunch," he reminded him, and as the cook frantically burst into action, and as the other people in the restaurant either began talking and eating again or bolted for the door while the coast was clear, he said to the man in gray, "It is no business of mine, but you are now unguarded in a place that seems hostile to you. I would suggest a hasty retreat. Those cowards"—he nodded toward the people pushing their way out the narrow doorway—"will provide you with excellent cover, at least for a short time."

Instead of taking his advice, the man visibly regained his composure and looked Wang up and down appreciatively, then said, "I have a better idea. You are very fast, faster than Kashigi here"—he nudged the dead man in the blue suit with his toe—"and faster than that mercenary scum over there. I need a new bodyguard and can pay well for the service. Would you be interested?"

The idea of being a bodyguard instead of an assassin had its appeal. Preserve rather than kill, protect rather than endanger . . . it might be an interesting change of pace. "Let us discuss this over lunch," Wang said. He held out his hand to the cook, who immediately scooped his octopus stir-fry into a bowl for him. "Make another for my friend, Mr.—" Wang looked over at his new acquaintance.

"Fuji," said the man, his eyes flicking away for a second. Wang knew he was lying even without turning to see the film advertisement on the wall that the man had read the name from. Wang also knew that the man knew he knew, and that he had intended him to know. It was a test.

12

"Very good." Wang turned again to the cook. "Make a bowl for my friend, Mr. Fuji. Quick, quick, photo finish!" The cook rushed to obey, and Wang led his prospective employer to a table where he had a good view of the entire restaurant. Hi Fat's was much quieter—and much emptier—than before. The two dead men were very quiet indeed, though Wang noticed that the one he had killed was dripping blood onto the floor. He had thrown too hard; the shuriken hadn't stopped in time to seal the entry wound. Sloppy, sloppy. Master Shoji would have him practicing with tomatoes for hours if he saw that. He hoped Fuji wouldn't notice.

"So, Mr. ASA 400, do you know why someone would want to kill you?"

"Oh yes," said Fuji. "I'm vice president of acquisitions for Zilla Enterprises. There must be at least a dozen other corporations who would love to keep me from acquiring their holdings. To say nothing of ambitious subordinates eager to make points with their masters."

"Ah, business," Wang said. That was all he needed to know. He didn't want to get involved in a personal vendetta, but business was fine. Business was about as impersonal as you got, at least for an underling, and Wang was under no illusion that he would be anything else. He controlled this first meeting because he had saved a man's life and because the man wanted something from him, but if he accepted the offer he would be an employee and from that point on he would be expected to act with deference and respect. That was fine, too. Wang could act any way that was

13

required of him so long as he understood the necessity of it.

And Zilla Enterprises, that was a stroke of fortune. Nothing like accidentally stumbling into a position with one of the largest multinational corporations in the world. Wang suspected a loyal employee would receive many extra forms of compensation besides simply yen in the bank, not the least of which was the advancement of his own reputation.

He argued money anyway, or tried to, but Fuji simply agreed to the first ridiculously high wage that Wang asked for, and he was suddenly employed.

He performed his first duty instantly. "Cook," he growled, and as if by magic the chef appeared from behind the counter with another steaming bowl of stir-fry for Mr. Fuji. Fuji looked surprised that Wang had remembered, but he settled in and ate while Wang did the same. If he had known Wang he would have been less surprised. One of the first rules any good warrior knew was to keep your energy stores in good supply. No fighter of Wang's experience would ever skip a meal when it was available.

Wang performed his second duty just outside the restaurant. Word had spread that Fuji was inside, and a trio of ninja, all dressed in black, waited insolently on the hood of the white limousine parked in the narrow street. The driver sat motionless inside, though it appeared that only fear held him immobile. Wang recognized all three ninja; they would not kill innocent bystanders or underlings unless it became necessary.

"Stand away from the car," Wang told them in a loud voice.

"Oho, Wang's a burglar alarm now!" one of them said.

"No, I'm a cleaning boy, and I don't want your blood to spoil the wax job."

They laughed. Wang took a few steps closer, careful to keep his body between them and his new employer, whom he was pleased to see followed confidently in his footsteps.

The three ninja stood up, and one casually pulled a long hamidashi knife from a scabbard at his side. "Unfortunate that you joined Zilla when you did," he said. "I would have enjoyed discussing our artform with you over sake."

"In another life, perhaps," Wang said, "but to minimize your disappointment, I promise I will teach you one new move today before you die."

The three ninja laughed again, then suddenly split apart like a springed mechanism when a person unscrews the wrong part. The one on the left glanced off the wall and came at Fuji; the one in the middle—the one who had spoken—came straight at Wang, and the third leaped up to the trunk of the limousine and pulled out a gun from beneath the folds of his gi.

Wang was so stunned by the sight of a ninja with a gleaming chrome revolver that he nearly forgot to defend his new charge. It wasn't yet instinct to protect anyone but himself. He remembered just in time, lashing out with a foot to snap the pole that held the awning over the door of the restaurant. Gravity (operating at only thirty-two feet per second squared, Master Shoji's voice whispered to him) would be too slow to drop the awning on the ninja, so Wang kicked a second time, breaking off a section of pipe, then a third with the flat of his foot to send the loose section flying into the ninja's stomach. It didn't penetrate, but internal injuries would put him out of the fight.

Wang had had to bend sideways to do that; the one who had come directly for him now had a straight run at Fuji. Wang straightened back up, tilted on over with the same motion, and let his own aikuchi dagger slide out of its wrist sheath as he raised his arm. The ninja's hamidashi was aimed for Fuji now instead of Wang; in the amount of time it took him to redirect his blow, Wang had already made the first of the three cuts that would disembowel him.

Out of the corner of his eye Wang could see the ninja with the gun squeeze the trigger. The barrel of the gun was just a tiny round circle with a hole in it, which meant it was aimed straight at Wang. Good, that meant Fuji was safe. Wang let the momentum of the nearer ninja add to his own strength and pull him aside just as the gun went off, and a bullet zinged off the paving stones behind him. Aiie! Bullets were fast. Too fast to deflect with his fingers, surely. Fortunately it still took a normal-speed person to fire them or Wang would have lost his job right there.

Fuji had ducked back into Hi Fat's again. Good; he was smart as well as confident in Wang's abilities. By eliminating himself as a target, he had allowed Wang greater choice in how to handle the situation.

"I promised to show you something new," he said to the ninja whose weight was now mostly supported by Wang's aikuchi in his belly. "Here is how to use a body as a shield." Wang knocked the ninja's hamidashi loose just in case he had any strength left to use

it, then lifted the man's body in the air and walked
with it toward the one with the gun. He was careful to
keep his own body hidden at all times behind the
other, but he suspected that the ninja on the car
wouldn't shoot his own companion in the back. He
was wrong in that assumption; he felt three solid
impacts and the man he carried shuddered and fell
limp, but the bullets didn't penetrate through him to
Wang.

"Time for another trick," Wang said. "Time to
learn how to fly." And with that he flung the body at
the gunman. It never connected—the man on the car
was a ninja, after all, even if he carried a gun—but
dodging the flying dead man did put him off balance
for a moment, and when Wang jostled the bumper of
the limousine with his foot, that finished the job. For
just a second the gunman had to concentrate on
keeping his balance rather than killing Wang, and that
was all the time Wang needed.

A leap and a kick sent the gun flying in a glittering
silver arc that ended across the street with a crash of
glass and a curse as a shopkeeper found a new item in
his window display. The ninja jumped back before
Wang could kick again, and now the width of the
limousine separated them. Not a problem; Wang
leaped over the trunk, twisting around in midair to
strike feet first. Of course the assassin didn't wait to
be struck, but he failed to dodge the knife that Wang
threw at the last instant into the spot where he would
have to move to avoid Wang's feet. The aikuchi
buried itself in the ninja's heart. He toppled toward
the car, but Wang pulled him back as he landed on his

17

feet. No sense getting blood on the wax job; somebody would have to clean it off even if that somebody wasn't Wang.

He walked back around the car and checked the ninja he had hit with the section of pipe. By his pasty white face and lack of breath, Wang guessed that his spleen or a major blood vessel had ruptured. He would trouble no one any more. Wang walked to the restaurant door and said to Fuji, who stood just inside, "Your car is ready now."

"Thank you," Fuji said, straightening his tie. They walked out of the restaurant without hindrance this time, and Wang opened the door for him. "I believe you are worth your price," Fuji said, looking at the carnage before he got into the car.

"I am worth twice that," Wang told him, "but I didn't want to sound greedy."

Chapter 3

The years with Zilla had been mostly good ones. Wang never learned Fuji's real name, nor, he suspected, the real name of anyone else in the corporation. Wang took to calling people whatever he wished, but always beginning with *F*: Fugu, Figit, Farthead—whatever suited the occasion. Fuji seemed amused by his conceit, except for the time when Wang referred to the Master himself, the shadowy head of the whole Zilla empire, as Father.

"Father is a term for God," Fuji said. "I will not have you referring to our leader as God Zilla."

Wang had backed down immediately, but in his secret heart he knew he had hit upon a fundamental truth. A man as powerful as Zilla no doubt thought of himself as a god, or at least the equal of one, and it probably annoyed him to no end that his name made such an unfortunate connotation so obvious. He would remember that. It was always useful to know how to enrage a person with a few words; that knowledge could come in handy if you ever needed to impair their judgment. Not that Wang could imagine a time when he would need to enrage the leader of the corporation he was sworn to protect, but it always paid to be prepared for any eventuality.

Life went on. Death went on, too. There were many attempts on Fuji's life and upon the lives of others in the corporation, and most times Wang was forced to kill the would-be assassins. Wang also learned that the life of a Shadow Warrior was not just about protection. He was often called upon to assist in business negotiations where force was required, or to clean up after a business deal went sour.

That seemed to happen more and more as the years went by. Whether international business was becoming more cutthroat in general or Zilla was simply adopting those tactics in particular was not apparent to Wang, nor did he really care except that it made his job more difficult. To stop in unannounced at a restaurant with Fuji the way his bodyguard had done on the day they met would be unthinkable now; first a goon-squad would have to be sent to soften up the restaurant owners, then an underling (one well under Fuji) would be sent to negotiate a buyout, and when his head came back in a box, Wang and at least five other Shadow Warriors would be dispatched to kill the owners and chase everyone else from the building except the cook and one waiter, who would be required to step over the bodies of the former owners while preparing a meal for their new ones.

It was entirely too much trouble for all concerned.

Fuji preferred to eat at home most nights now, and Wang was glad to keep him company.

That was not to last, however. A bodyguard as ruthlessly efficient as Wang could not go unnoticed in a corporation whose officers went through bodyguards as fast as Zilla's did. Wang soon found himself summoned into the presence of the great Zilla himself, who remained in shadow while Wang was seated on a stool with a spotlight trained in his eyes to prevent him from seeing the great patriarch's face. The two Shadow Warriors who had escorted him there stood on either side of him, arms crossed over their chests. An odd, musky smell permeated the room, which was large and echoing and sparsely furnished even by Japanese standards.

"Your service record is most impressive," a deep, gravelly voice said from the darkness.

"Yes, it is," Wang admitted.

"Modesty was not listed among your accomplishments," the voice said. "I'm glad to see that was not a careless omission." The gravelly rasping continued a few seconds longer. A chuckle.

"I didn't know modesty was required."

"Oh, never fear. It's not. Not in this business."

"Yours or mine?" Wang hoped to get a rise out of Zilla with that so he could learn more about the man's nature, and he wasn't disappointed.

"Your business *is* my business," the disembodied voice rasped, but a second later it said, "Wait, maybe that's 'my business is your business.' Damn, I can never remember which way it goes in cases like this." There was some whispering there in the dark as Zilla no doubt conferred with an advisor, then the voice said, "It doesn't matter. You work for me, that's the important bit. And I want you to work a bit closer from now on."

Wang was pretty sure he didn't want to get any closer to Zilla. In fact, something about that voice sent shivers up his spine. It was an instinctive reaction, originating from well below the conscious levels of his brain, and it made Wang decidedly uncomfortable. He would have taken a cut in pay to stay in Fuji's service if that was possible, but he knew there was no going back from here. If there was one thing he'd learned in his years of service to the organization, it was that nobody could turn down an offer from Zilla and live.

But perhaps Zilla could be convinced to rescind the offer. Wang leaned forward as if to listen more closely, and deliberately overbalanced his stool. He fell to the polished cedar floor with a solid thump, as clumsily as a drunkard, and the stool bounced away behind him.

"My apologies," Wang said, standing up and fumbling the stool upright again. He made a great show of adjusting its position before he settled his weight on it again, but as he did so he flexed his mighty gluteus maximus, the stool broke into pieces, and he wound up on the floor again.

"So sorry," he said again, floundering to stand up. "Just nervous, that's all. Won't happen again." But as he said that he stepped on one of the stool's legs and let it roll out from under his feet, sending him to the floor a third time.

Laughter erupted in the room, not only from Zilla but from the unseen advisor and from the two Shadow Warriors who had accompanied Wang into the audience chamber.

"Very amusing," Zilla said. "Not only are you a flawless fighter, but you can act as well. I like you. Step closer."

Embarrassed now, Wang walked forward. The shaft of light from behind Zilla slid up Wang's body, engulfed his head, and then he was beneath it. He squinted toward the source of the voice, but saw only a shadowy figure in a dark cloak with the hood drawn over his face.

"That's close enough," said Zilla. "In five or ten years, if you prove trustworthy, perhaps you can come closer. In the meantime, this is what you will see, and this is what you will protect."

Wang would *have* to get closer sometimes, he thought, if only in an elevator or a car. Unless . . . "Do you never leave this room?" Wang asked.

"Never," said Zilla.

That would account for the smell, thought Wang, but he wisely said nothing.

Guarding a man who never left his inner sanctum, which was itself guarded by hundreds of others in various levels of security that extended outward for miles, was not exactly an exciting job. Fortunately Wang was only on duty half the day, but the twelve hours when he stood watch were the longest hours of his life. He spent his time studying the audience chamber, familiarizing himself with every detail.

Zilla had decorated with military museum pieces. Suits of yoroi, the leather and bamboo armor from a previous age, stood on stands along the side walls.

Menpo, the face guards that also served as fright masks, hung from pegs beside the armor. Black lacquer kate racks held paired long and short swords.

There were non-military touches as well. A small Buddhist shrine occupied the space behind Zilla's dais. Bonsai flanked Zilla's chair. Wang was amused to see that it was not pine or maple, but fern that Zilla chose to hold in perpetual miniature.

Wang also studied the room's architecture, not in simple admiration of its style, which was unimpressive, but so he could learn every knot in the wood and every nick in the stones that might affect a battle if one were ever fought here. He calculated where the weak spots in the roof beams were, which floorboards could be dislodged in an emergency to provide impromptu weapons, and which wall panels would reveal electrical wiring that he could use to electrocute or simply strangle an opponent.

And while he examined the room, he listened. Advisors drifted in and out like wraiths, bearing reports and leaving with orders. All their business was conducted in whispers, but a Shadow Warrior trained his ears as well as the rest of his body. Wang would methodically blank out every other noise in the room, every echo and sniff and scuff of foot, until the only sounds to reach his brain were Zilla's raspy words.

Even that was not enough, but again Master Shoji's training came to Wang's aid. The room was elliptical, the roof vaulted, and Zilla's dais was near one end; that put his head near the focus of the ellipse. "An ellipse has two foci!" Shoji had once intoned, and while Wang had made no sense of it at the time, now he understood. He positioned himself at the other focus, the one near the doorway opposite Zilla, and sure enough, the room's walls and ceiling reflected the sound straight to him, amplifying it in the process.

And in that way Lo Wang learned that his master was in league with the forces of darkness.

Chapter 4

YOU ONLY DIE TWICE

It had been clear right from the start that Zilla wanted to rule the world. Wang had no problem with that ambition. Somebody had to do the job, and it might as well be someone who could do it efficiently. Zilla was nothing if not efficient. Wang felt the first pangs of distressed conscience only when he overheard the method Zilla planned to use to realize his power-hungry scheme.

The demon came out of nowhere. Wang had admittedly not been paying the closest attention to the goings-on in the audience chamber, not after many weeks of monotony, but he would have noticed if the door were opened. It wasn't. At least not the main door. Zilla and one of his equally shadowy associates had been arguing about whether or not they could muster enough warriors for a particularly difficult hostile takeover when Zilla had suddenly said, "Show me. I've heard nothing but talk from

26

you up to this point; show me that you can summon one. Just one."

The associate had nodded, then whispered something Wang couldn't catch even with the elliptical geometry of the room to amplify it. He held his hands together in a mystic hand position with two fingers upward, two crossed, and the rest curled, then he drew them upward and swept them out and down. There was a ripping sound, as if someone had torn a bedsheet in half, and another shadowy figure stepped out as if through a doorway to stand before the one who had made the gestures. This one was not merely cloaked in dark cloth; it appeared to be *made* of shadow. Light could not find purchase enough to reflect back from it. It was a man-shaped hole in the air, and an aura of menace permeated the room the moment it appeared.

Wang had been slouching lazily at his post. He snapped instantly to full alertness, but he didn't allow a single muscle twitch to betray his heightened awareness. He had foolishly allowed his attention to wander; let this creature of night think he was still distracted. He listened carefully as the summoner said to Zilla, "This is one of the tame ones. You wouldn't want a real warrior here, believe me."

"Why not? Can't you control them? They're no good to us if they're uncontrollable."

"Oh, they're controllable. They obey orders very well, so long as those orders are to kill something. But they're rather like nuclear bombs; even if they don't go off, it's not healthy to spend a lot of time near them."

"I see. Well then, what does this tame one do? You

haven't yet proven to me that you can conjure more than a three-dimensional silhouette."

"It can kill your bodyguard," said the whispery voice of the summoner.

Zilla laughed. "I rather doubt that. Wang, what do you think? Can this shadow kill you?"

Wang straightened up. So much for the advantage of surprise. "I certainly hope not," he said.

"So do I. You've been a loyal retainer for many years. On the other hand, these night creatures charge considerably less for their services, and Ginnjon here tells me they eat the bodies of their enemies so there's practically no food budget as long as you keep them fighting. I'm thinking of switching over to them exclusively. If they prove themselves in action, of course."

"That would be a mistake," said Wang.

It was the first time he had offered unsolicited advice to anyone at Zilla Enterprises since Fuji had hired him. The great Zilla himself laughed again and said, "Why is that?" which was what Wang was hoping he would do. The more time he could take to study this bizarre phantom, the better he would fare in the inevitable battle. Wang had no illusion that he would escape a fight with it, and he didn't particularly mind that, but it always helped to know what he was fighting.

"It would be a mistake," he said, "because you are allying yourself with a power that is greater than you, but which does not have your interests in mind. Those who deal with the forces of darkness always become pawns in their evil schemes. Even the great Zilla. If you use them as your bodyguards, you will find them to be your executioners the first time you try to cross their true master."

The phantom never moved, never blinked, never breathed. Wang could learn nothing from it like this. He stepped closer to see how it would react to that.

"Well reasoned," Zilla said. "Except for one flaw in your logic. You have made the false assumption that I am powerless to protect myself." Zilla extended a finger out from the folds of his sable robe. The end of it glowed red, and a spot on the wall to Wang's right exploded in a shower of flaming splinters. Wang flinched, and he noticed that the phantom did, too. He had no idea what Zilla had done. He had seen no missile, no tongue of flame, nothing but the glowing finger—actually a glowing spot *beside* the finger, now that he thought about it—and the explosion. This was something new. Even so, Wang said, "Your weapons may protect your body, but nothing can protect your karma from its contact with these creatures."

"My karma is not your worry," said Zilla. He turned to his underling. "Let's see what it can do."

The summoner whispered a sharp command and the phantom sprang instantly into action, leaping straight for Wang. It didn't run, it just leaped, one long, low arc covering the five or six steps it should have taken to reach its target. But Wang was not there to meet it. He stepped aside as nimbly as the creature had jumped, drew his sword from over his shoulder, and spun around to slice it neatly in two while it was still in the air.

Except the phantom seemed to flow around the blade, like a silk scarf around a maiden's arm. Wang

29

felt only the faintest hint of resistance against the sword, but he heard a startled exclamation from a voice that sounded like a cat in heat and then the creature was past. It landed on its feet, apparently unharmed, and lashed out with a front kick at Wang's midsection. Wang pulled back and the foot merely glanced off his ribs, but it felt as if he had been splashed with molten lead.

What was this thing? None of the martial forms that Wang had learned were designed to fight something nonhuman. Wang tried, but a side kick to its legs didn't topple it, a rising punch to its sternum didn't paralyze its heart, and each time he touched it he burned in agony for his trouble.

The sword had at least done something. Wang whipped it back and forth through the animated patch of night, the blade singing in the air with each pass, and was rewarded by fresh howls of cat-voiced rage. The creature backed away, and Wang pressed the attack, thinking furiously what else he could do. The thing should have died a dozen times over by now, but the sword was obviously just an inconvenience.

Wang got no chance to try anthing else. The phantom suddenly stopped retreating and let Wang slice away at it, then slowly, mewling with pain the entire time, it advanced directly into Wang's flashing sword. Long before it reached his hand, the sword grew too hot to hold. Wang flung it away from him, noting where it stuck in the wall in case he needed it again, and leaped back to give himself more time. The phantom leaped after him and Wang let it come, grabbing its head and giving it a savage twist, then adding his own strength to the creature's own momentum and throwing it halfway across the chamber.

His hands burned from the contact, even though it hadn't felt as if he'd actually grasped anything more substantial than a cobweb. He certainly hadn't broken the creature's neck. It landed where its own leap had sent it and took its time turning around to face Wang again. And now Wang could see its eyes. He expected to see them glow red, but they were a pale blue, like the blue of ice on a pond in midwinter. They pulsed, brighter, dimmer, brighter—then flashed so bright that Wang was momentarily blinded. His entire front side burned with the same fire he had felt before, but now Wang realized it wasn't fire; it was cold, cold so intense it *felt* like fire as it sucked the heat out of his body.

But there was real fire in the room. Wang flung a handful of caltrops to the floor to slow the phantom down while he went for the smoldering spot on the wall where Zilla had demonstrated his strength, but the phantom stepped right through the sharpened points without pausing. Wang moved toward it, shifted right, feinted left, then leaped to the right around his opponent and sprinted to the burned spot. Two strips of wood leaned outward from the blast point, their ends trailing smoke. Wang ripped them loose and blew on them to get the fire going again, but the phantom didn't give him time. The embers had turned bright orange, but hadn't burst into flame yet when it jumped at him again, so Wang flung one at the dark form's midsection, then shoved the other into its face and stirred.

It shrieked in true pain for the first time and pulled

away. Wang's weapon had already grown dimmer, but he pressed the attack, shoving the hot ember that remained into the dark body again and again. It worked beautifully at first, burning actual gaps in the creature's insubstantial shape, but the intense cold quickly extinguished the coals and Wang was left with only a charred stick in his hand.

The phantom was injured, but Wang could not tell how badly. He looked past it to where Zilla and his associate watched as they might have watched a horse race they hadn't bet on. Interested, yet impassive. But was the underling so impassive? No. Lines in his robe betrayed muscles in tension beneath. Things weren't going as well as he had expected.

Good. For the moment Wang had the advantage. But what could he do to keep it that way? He had no more fire, and no way to make any. Not unless . . . He thought it over in the few seconds of respite he had earned for himself. What would it hurt? His master had turned on him already; there was really nothing left to lose.

"You know, Zilla," he said, dodging to stay away from the phantom, "the way you treat your employees, a person might think you had a god complex. What do you think? God Zilla? Does have a nice ring to it, doesn't it?"

Zilla tilted his head, obviously puzzled, but he didn't fire his weapon. Damn. Trust the guy to be pun-impaired. So much for that long-held piece of useless knowledge.

Time for plan B. Quick as thought, Wang shifted the flat stick in his hand until he gripped it in the middle, then flicked it toward Zilla, spinning it hard along its long axis as he did. The stick buzzed like a huge insect as its fluttering edges caught the air, and it wobbled up and down erratically in its flight toward the surprised Master.

This time Zilla did what Wang wanted: he instinctively fired at the stick. A man who sat in a padded chair all day couldn't practice enough with whatever weapon he hid under his cloak; it took several shots before he hit the stick. Explosions from the wild shots burst forth all along the wall beside the phantom, and when it flinched away, Wang rushed toward them and ripped free a double handful of burning wall. He flung a few firebrands at the phantom, then attacked again with what remained.

The creature of darkness wailed and sizzled, and more gaps appeared in its silhouette until it looked like a moth-eaten scroll, but still it didn't die. When Wang's last torch flickered out it advanced on him again, and its freezing touch hurt just as badly as it had before.

"Impressive," Zilla rumbled. Wang knew he would not be able to trick him into firing his weapon again, not unless the phantom were to attack Zilla, and he couldn't think of a way to make it do that.

But maybe he could make it *go for* Zilla . . . The thing seemed to rush mindlessly at Wang, always with the direct assault, even now as Wang dodged and weaved frantically from side to side in an attempt to confuse it. If he could position himself behind Zilla, maybe the thing would rush them both.

The thought was the deed. Zilla did fire his weapon

again as Wang rushed past only a foot or so away, but Wang was far too fast for him to hit. He spun around to see if the phantom had taken the bait, but was dismayed to find that it apparently had just enough intelligence to go around an obstacle rather than straight through it.

But what if it couldn't see the obstacle? Wang backed up a few more paces until he reached the spotlight that Zilla used to blind people with, flipped it on, and trained the beam straight on the black phantom.

The result was not what he expected. The phantom cried out with a howl that rose in pitch until it seemed it should shatter eardrums, but the howl cut off just as Wang clapped his hands over his ears. It was a good thing he had them protected, though, because the explosion that followed would have deafened him just as readily.

There was nothing left of the phantom, not even a smudge of soot. Zilla and the summoner of darkness blinked and butted their heads with the heels of their hands in the classic but fruitless pose of people trying to knock loose the ringing in their ears. Wang turned the spotlight directly on them, then stood a pace to the side and waited for them to come to their senses.

"Turn that damned thing off," Zilla growled at last. Even now, only a pair of glowing red eyes marked the face beneath the hood.

"Turn it off yourself," Wang said. "I quit."

Zilla jerked his head back as if he'd been physically slapped. "What did you say?"

"I said, *I quit!*" Wang shouted, just to make sure Zilla heard him this time.

"You can't quit Zilla Enterprises. Not alive."

"Watch me."

Zilla stuck his weapon out from under his robe again, and now Wang could see a shiny lens at the end of it. A laser, then. Wang had heard of them, and had suspected that's what it was. He let Zilla fire it, and at the last moment he pulled the spotlight down to be in the beam's path. The bulb exploded from the sudden heat, but the reflector didn't: a wide, diffuse laser beam shot straight back at Zilla and the other man, blinding them even more effectively than the spotlight had. It would take them days to recover from that.

"You have treated me poorly and you have loosed the forces of darkness upon me," Wang said. "For the third and final time I tell you: I quit."

He let the ruined spotlight crash to the floor and walked past Zilla and the other man to the door, stopping to wrench his sword free from the wall on his way. At the door he turned and said, "You have called shame upon this house, and that creature you summoned has nearly dishonored the name Shadow Warrior, but I will keep that name for myself even so. I, Lo Wang, am the true Shadow Warrior." He plucked two of his own favorite four-pointed style of shuriken from his belt and flung them almost casually in Zilla's direction, where they stuck in the arms of his chair and pinned his sleeves to the wood.

"I could have killed you," Wang said. "I have that option, and I have that right, but I choose to spare your miserable life. It is sufficient that I turn my back upon you and your entire organization. But I warn you, do not darken the world's doorstep with these creatures again or I will come back and finish the job." And with that, he opened the door and stepped out into a new life.

Chapter 5

It lasted about a week. He was in a crowded Tokyo bar, celebrating his newfound freedom with a friendly geisha, when the first hint of trouble came.

As usual, it arrived in the form of someone spoiling for a fight. Two drunken neighborhood gangsters, yakuza, staggered into the bar, jostling their way through the thick press of people around the karaoke stage, and shoved a couple of aged neo-samurai away from the bar. The neo-samurai grumbled, but they hadn't gotten old by defending their honor against every village idiot who came along, so they didn't fight for their places. Even when the disappointed bullies made fun of them, calling them cowards and peasants in loud voices that carried all through the bar, the neo-samurai merely drank their sake and left.

Wang should have left as well, but he had a table in the corner away from the bar, and the girl he shared it with, Kabuki, was too pretty. Wang had been celibate too long to allow anything less than an assassination attempt to cut short his enjoyment of her charms.

He had lucked into her company when the electronics manufacturer who had arranged for an evening's companion had failed to show up to meet her. She had looked lost and lonely, so he had introduced himself and offered to buy her a drink. She had accepted, then after they'd gotten to know one another a little bit she had sung for him, completely outclassing the amateurs who warbled foreign songs to which they couldn't pronounce the lyrics. She had laughed at his jokes and she had oohed and aahed in all the right spots when he described some of his exploits as a muscle man for Zilla. She was perfect in every way, and for tonight, at least, she was Wang's.

Behind her, someone sang an off key lyric to an American song. Even though Wang's English wasn't all that good, he seriously doubted if the original artist had written a line that went "There's a warm wind blowing the stars around," but he wasn't in a complaining mood. He was free, he was happy, he had a beautiful woman's attention—

And then a spray of warm sake splashed across her white kimono and she screamed and jumped up from the table, dabbing at the wet silk with a napkin. Wang stood up, overturning his chair in the process, and turned to demand an apology from the clumsy oaf who had done it. It was, of course, the two troublemakers from the bar. They grinned at Wang, waiting to see what he would do.

"Apologize to Kabuki," Wang said quietly.

For answer, they both pulled tantos—short knives

with wide hand guards—from their belts. One made a slash toward Wang's face, which he easily dodged.

"Any last words?" Wang asked.

"Huh?" asked one.

"That is a stupid last word," Wang said, but he didn't give the idiot a chance to pick another. Faster than the eye could follow, he plucked the tanto from the yakuza's outstretched hand, then took the empty sake cup from his other hand, turned it so the base of the cup faced the kid's lips, pulled his mouth open, and shoved the cup down his throat. It all happened in the blink of an eye; to everyone else in the bar it probably looked like the yakuza had swallowed wrong and began to choke, if it looked like anything at all. He clutched at the lump in his throat, pushing at it more and more frantically as he ran out of air, but no sound escaped. Nor did any oxygen reach the few neurons he called a brain, and in a few short seconds he collapsed to the floor.

His companion looked from Wang to his fallen buddy, whom he apparently thought was clowning around, but as the seconds dragged on and he didn't get up, the one still standing finally said, "Hey."

"An equally stupid epitaph," said Wang. This one wasn't carrying a sake cup; Wang had to provide his own, but it worked just as well as the first one. "Compliments of the house," he said when the choking was over.

He turned back to Kabuki, congratulating himself on taking care of the situation with a minimum of fuss, but a little nagging voice at the back of his mind was warning him that something was still wrong. That had been way too easy, even for street gang members, the voice said, but Wang wasn't listening. If he hadn't already had a dozen cups of sake by the time he'd sacrificed his cup, and if the woman across from him wasn't the most beautiful woman he had ever met, he might have given it more thought, but he wasn't in an analytical mood.

She was still dabbing at her kimono. "Are you all right?" he asked her.

"Fine," she said. "Those clumsy oafs ruined my gown, though. I'll never get the stain out unless I can soak it in cold water right away." The silk was nearly translucent to begin with; where the sake had wet it her breasts showed through in exquisite detail. Wang could see her heartbeat punctuate the motion from her quick, excited breaths.

"I have a place nearby where you could change out of it," Wang offered helpfully.

"Oh, do you?" she asked, batting her eyelashes. "That would be wonderful." She reached out her delicate right hand to Wang, who took it in his own muscled fingers to help her through the crowded bar. He couldn't believe his luck. Perhaps he should extract the sake cups from the two unconscious troublemakers' throats as thanks for providing him with the opportunity.

Or not. It was their problem if they couldn't hold their sake.

Then the poisoned needle she had concealed in her palm bit into his hand and his whole body erupted in pain. It was some kind of neurotoxin, it had to be, one that spread like an explosion from the point of contact. It hurt worse than the dark phantom's icy grip, worse than a sword bite, worse than anything Wang had ever felt before.

Yet his shame was nearly as debilitating as the neurotoxin. He had been set up. The two men he had killed had been kamikaze decoys sent to distract him while Kabuki slipped the deadly needle out of her kimono. So simple, yet so effective, for Wang had fallen for it like a rank amateur. After all these years, he had let his guard down once and that was all it took.

"Who . . . ?" he managed to croak as the fiery pain gave over to numbness that spread like frostbite up his arms and into his body.

"Who do you think, shadow man?" she replied, jabbing him again in the hand with her needle just to make sure she'd gotten him.

"Zilla," Wang said, and the look in her eyes told him he was right.

He teetered sideways, but caught himself on the edge of the table. There had been enough poison in the needle to kill half a dozen men, but Lo Wang was no ordinary man. Of the many things Master Shoji had taught him, the most difficult had been the control of those parts of the body that aren't usually subject to control. Wang had learned how to make his heart stop, how to hold his breath for half an hour, how to stop the sensation of pain no matter how great—and he had learned how to constrict the flow of blood to each of the veins and arteries in his body. What the toxin couldn't reach, it couldn't kill.

Wang shut out the pain with hardly any difficulty. "Pain is for the weak," he had always said, though he usually meant it sarcastically. Now he was just glad he

could stop it so he could concentrate on the real task;
keeping the neurotoxin from spreading to anything
vital. Wang could control his body, but he couldn't
bring it back from the dead.

His outward appearance didn't betray the great
internal struggle that raged through him, but Kabuki
grew worried anyway as seconds ticked past and Wang
didn't collapse. She jabbed at him again. This time he
jerked his hand away before she could inject any more
poison into his system, and when she tried to follow
his hand he batted her arm aside, breaking both the
radius and the ulna. Clumsy, clumsy, he thought
through the fog of effort. If he'd been in good form he
could have taken it off cleanly at the elbow.

He didn't have time for niceties. The toxin was still
spreading. Wang knew he had only a few minutes of
consciousness left, and he couldn't afford to spend
any more time on Kabuki. It was time to take his own
advice to Fuji, given so long ago, and make a clean
getaway while he had the chance. Kabuki had collapsed into her chair, cradling her broken arm in her
other hand, and Wang left her there, lurching through
the crowd toward the door. People laughed, thinking
he was drunk, and a few kind souls even helped him
stagger out into the night.

He was becoming disoriented. He would never
make it the three blocks to the apartment he had
rented over the tailor's shop. That would be the first
place Zilla's agents would look for him anyway. He
needed to find shelter somewhere closer, somewhere
he could hide from the inevitable follow-up team
Kabuki would call in to finish him off. He should have
killed her so she couldn't sound the alarm. Stupid. He

should have killed Zilla, too, when he'd had the chance. He had grown too compassionate during his period of inactivity. He vowed never to make that mistake again.

It was entirely possible that he would never do anything again, like see the dawn or even take another dozen breaths, but Wang pushed himself down the street by sheer will power, gripping store fronts for support as he went.

Store fronts. He realized he was being stupid. There were hiding places everywhere, and most of them wouldn't be checked until morning. Slowly, his nerves refusing to respond to anything but the strongest command, and every move that he did make generating fresh waves of pain that he had to blank out, he moved to the middle of the block where an alley led back to the loading docks. He went halfway down the alley, then leaned up against the wall next to a garbage can and pressed his back flat to the cool bricks. He lifted one foot, then slammed it backward against the wall.

Kinetic energy equalled one half mass times velocity squared. Good thing his feet were far more massive than a hand, because he couldn't get much velocity out of them tonight. This was a brute force situation. The wall shuddered under his blow, and a crack ran upward past his head. He kicked again and knocked a half dozen bricks inside. A third kick widened the hole enough to crawl through.

Wang listened. No alarms sounded. Shop owners always wired the doors and windows; nobody thought to wire the walls. He bent down and crawled through the hole, then turned around and pulled the garbage can up against it to block it from view. He shoved the bricks back into place from the inside, then brushed away the crumbled evidence that remained and leaned back against the wall.

He took a moment to control his quivering muscles. Nerves burned like hot wires all through his body, conquering his best effort to ignore their pain signals. The toxin was spreading fast despite his lowered heartbeat and constricted arteries. If Wang was going to survive this, he needed to shut his circulation down to the bare minimum and give his body time to fight it, and for that he needed to find a place where he would be safe for days.

He looked around at the shadowy shapes in the store he had broken into. Vase-like silhouettes about a foot high stood on every horizontal surface. Light from outside shined through them, revealing irregular dark blobs suspended in liquid. They looked very biological. Eye of newt and wing of bat? Pickled goat brains? Wang stepped closer to one and inspected it carefully, then burst out laughing despite his agony. The place sold lava lamps, cheap plastic knock-offs for tourists.

Wang had busted his way into the back of the store. By the looks of the clutter, this wasn't just an outlet; this must be the place where they actually assembled the lamps. And shipped them to America. There was a large wooden crate in the middle of the floor, packed full and ready to go.

America, Wang thought. Land of opportunity. Yes, America would do fine.

He pried up the top of the crate and began removing lamps, stacking them back on the shelves around him so there wouldn't be any obvious evidence that someone had emptied the box. When he had excavated a large enough space for himself to fit in, he arranged the fibrous packing material to make a soft bed and climbed inside, careful to distribute his weight so he wouldn't break any of the lamps beneath him. It wasn't difficult; a Shadow Warrior was trained to sleep on raw eggs if necessary without breaking them. He pulled the lid down with a sharp jerk that seated the nails back in their holes without—he hoped—leaving any of their heads protruding above.

It was pitch dark and stuffy. Wang stiffened a finger and punched an air hole through the wood near his head. One would be sufficient; he planned to lower his metabolism to that of a hibernating Honshu bear until his body had cleaned away the toxin.

Now would be a good time to begin. He could feel it hammering away at his brain, already killing off nerve cells. He needed to slow everything down, give his body time to attack and remove the alien molecules.

Concentration was difficult with the unblockable pain racking his body, but Wang gritted his teeth and began the yoga techniques he had learned as a boy. Relax one part of his body at a time, starting with the toes. Relax the little toe on his left foot, relax it completely, relax, relax, even if Master Shoji is standing on it with cleated sandals. Now the next toe, and the next. All the way up his body to the brain.

Somewhere along the way he lost consciousness, but he had practiced this so many times that instinct continued the job. A few minutes later his breathing became almost imperceptible. If anyone had stumbled across him in this condition, they would have been sure he was dead.

They would have been wrong. Down inside, a tiny spark of being continued to glow, a warm spot of potential like the lump of plutonium at the heart of a nuclear bomb. Waiting patiently for the right moment to explode into life again.

Chapter 6

Wang felt a jolt. A loud voice, muffled by the wooden crate, said, "Hey, careful with that, you moron! Can't you read? It says Fragile here."

Another voice said, "It says squiggle, squiggle, funny hat on a house. I'm supposed to know that means fragile?"

"Damn right you do if you're going to work unloading Japanese cargo."

"Why the hell can't they use English like everybody else?" the second voice complained.

Wang smiled in the dark interior of the crate. Ah yes, he was in America.

And he didn't hurt. He was stiff from not moving for so long and weak as a kitten from lack of food, but his body had eliminated the neurotoxin. Considering how he'd felt when he'd climbed into this packing crate coffin, he felt in excellent health.

He heard a loud *beep, beep, beep*, then felt another

thump. He braced himself while the stevedores jock-
eyed the crate onto a forklift and wheeled it into a
truck, which, by the steadily decreasing echo, they
apparently packed full. Wang waited until he heard
the doors at the end of the trailer slam closed, then
he pushed up on the lid of his crate until the nails
squealed and gave way. There were advantages to
being in a box marked Fragile; he was at the top
rather than the bottom of a stack. It was pitch dark
inside the trailer, but a Shadow Warrior didn't need
light to find his way. Wang climbed out of the crate,
watching his head against the close ceiling, and felt
for clues. More crates on three sides and a thin metal
wall on the fourth. The ceiling was the same thin
metal; he made a fist and punched through it, letting
in a stream of sunlight so bright after his days in
darkness that it made him squint. That in turn made
him sneeze.

He froze, listening for signs that anyone had heard
him, but nobody opened the trailer door. The oily,
wet scent of a busy harbor came through the hole. It
was still the freshest air Wang had smelled in days; he
breathed deep, then crawled across the tops of the
boxes and examined the door, but he quickly discovered that it was not designed to be opened from
inside. Stupid design; what if a man were trapped in
there? Wang considered waiting in the truck until it
delivered him to its destination, but he had no idea
where that might be. He needed food and water and
he needed it now, not after another day or two in
transit. So he climbed back across the crate tops to the
spot where he had made the hole, grasped the ragged

metal edges, and ripped back a flap of it large enough to climb through.

He stuck his head out cautiously, but nobody had paid any attention to what little noise he had made. Not in a shipyard full of cranes and forklifts. He climbed on out of the hole, walked to the front of the truck, jumped down onto the cab, and from there to the hood and finally to the ground. There was no truck driver, but a forklift operator driving by looked curiously at Wang, no doubt wondering about his bare chest and skintight pants, the sword over his shoulder and the weapons belt at his waist. Wang smiled and waved at him, then sauntered off toward a row of parked cars as if he had that destination in mind all along. With a little shrug the forklift operator waved back and drove on.

Some of the cars probably held food, Wang reasoned. Candy bars, rice cakes—something edible. He couldn't get close enough to search them, however, before an enormous black and brown dog in the back of a pickup truck started barking furiously at him.

"Dame," Wang commanded it, but the dog kept barking. "Damare!" Still it barked. Oh, of course. He was in America now. He tried to recall the right word. "Not!" he said to the dog. "Hold." It continued to bark. Either he had not used the right words, or the dog was poorly trained. It lunged at him when he came closer, barking madly through jaws large enough to take a man's arm off. This animal was dangerous. Someone could get hurt. So Wang reached out and hit it alongside its head with the edge of his hand. He felt skull bones crush and the dog fell into the bed of the pickup, blood gushing out its mouth. Annoying creature. Wang hoped America wasn't full of them.

He turned his attention to the cab of the truck, but saw no evidence of food. Nor in the car next to the pickup, nor in the four cars beyond that. He looked around to see if there might be any more obvious place to find sustenance. Nothing.

The scent of fresh blood wafted over from the back of the truck. Wang paused, considering. It wasn't his usual fare, but what he really needed most was protein, and there was plenty of it there.

He walked back and pulled the dog's body from the back of the pickup, snapping the chain that had held it from running away, and carried it farther into the parking lot, finally settling down between two rusted-out American cars. There he took out his aikuchi and gutted the dog, tossing the entrails into the back seat of one of the cars through its busted-out back window. Then he began carving big chunks of meat from its flanks and haunches.

He had had better, but this wasn't bad. Not bad at all. Tasted a bit like chicken.

He spent the rest of the day exploring the dockyard, learning where the offices were and where the gates were and where he could hide when he needed to. From the sign at the front gate he learned that he was in Los Angeles, and from the top of one of the warehouses he saw that the city went on for miles in every direction. He supposed he would have to explore at least part of it soon, but for today the dockyard was sufficient.

He spent the night in another packing crate, this

one not destined for anywhere, and in the morning he set out looking for a job and a home. That proved even easier than it had in Japan. Just like back home, all Wang had to do was kill the right person at the right time, and suddenly he was in high demand. The difference in California was that nobody had any artistry in their killing, so Wang stood out like a cat in an aviary.

It happened shortly after dawn. Wang was still hanging around the dockyards, hoping someone else would bring their dog to work with them, when a white car pulled into the parking lot. Its driver, a little man in a dark blue suit, parked it in the handicapped spot near the office door and rushed inside, carrying a briefcase with papers sticking out from three sides. Shouting came from the office, and Wang grew curious enough to peek in the open window and listen to the argument. His English wasn't good enough to allow him to catch all of it, but it sounded like a blackmail situation to him. The little man was making the demands, waving a sheaf of papers in his hand as he did so, and a bigger man with a sterner, meaner voice kept telling him he couldn't do what he asked. Finally the big man told the little man to get lost, and the little man blustered toward the door with his briefcase, threatening to close down the entire shipyard for that.

"Go right ahead," the big man shouted after him. "Put two hundred people out of work because we don't have big enough idiot labels on our forklifts. See how that sits with the unemployment office."

Wang disliked this imperious little weasel. Instead of slipping away around the side of the building, he stood up and walked toward the door, timing it so the two of them collided head on. Wang flexed his stomach muscles at just the right moment and propelled the little man back into the office, flailing wildly for balance.

"And that's another violation right there!" the little man shouted. "You should have a convex mirror above the door so people can see if somebody else is coming!"

"So sorry," Wang said, bowing an infinitesimally small, insolent bow. "Lo Wang look for job. Didn't see little whining man until too late."

The little man scrambled to his feet, his eyes bugging out from the insult and at the sight of Wang with his sword and wrist knife, plus the belt full of shuriken and kusari-fundo fighting chains. "Good God!" he said. "This man is armed. That's another violation!"

"Is not right to have arms?" Wang asked, hamming it up by flexing his biceps and putting on a good puzzled expression. "Lo Wang thinks arms would help in unloading ships, neh?"

The big man laughed. "You got that right, brother. You look like you could unload a ship all by yourself. Ever been a dockhand before?"

"No," Wang said. "I have been prescription—no, how you say . . . professional assassin all my life."

Both men's jaws dropped. "You're not kidding, are you?" the big one asked, and Wang could see the unspoken plea in the way his eyes flickered to the little man and then back to Wang.

They were the only three people in the office. Wang

casually closed the door. "I very good. Would you like I demonstrate?"

"No, you can't do that sort of thing here, no matter how good it would feel." The big man leered at the little one as he said that.

Wang had learned how to listen for the true meaning in people's words; this man's intent was clear as glass. Not only that, but by the way his hands clenched and unclenched, Wang could even tell what method he would like used.

"One should never hold in frustrations like you do," he told the man. "Very bad for you. Leads to heart and stomach disease. Here, I take care of whole problem for you."

He reached out and snatched the little man by his neck and lifted him up off the ground.

"No," said the big man, but it was clear he didn't mean it, so Wang wrapped both hands around the little man's neck and squeezed. The little man's head turned purple as a plum and his eyes bugged out like a goldfish's. His feet kicked back and forth annoyingly, so Wang clenched his fingers tighter until he felt the neck break, then he casually tossed the body to the floor.

"Holy shit, you snuffed him just like that," the big man whispered. "I've been wanting to do that for years."

"He not deserve it?" Wang asked. For a moment he worried that he might have killed an innocent man.

"Well yeah, but—but—we don't do things that way around here."

"Perhaps if you did you would have fewer digestive

53

problems," Wang told him. "This my gift to you, but I ask for favor in return. I seek job and somewhere to live."

He could see the man thinking it over. "Where are you from, anyway?" he asked.

"Fresh off boat from Japan," Wang answered.

"You got a green card? Passport?"

"I have what you see here." Wang held out his arms and turned once around.

"That seems to be plenty." The shipyard boss—at least that's what he seemed to be—rubbed his grizzled face and asked, "Are you as good at making bodies disappear as you are at making 'em bodies in the first place?"

Wang had seldom bothered to dispose of a body; the whole point of most assassinations was to advertise to the survivors that they could be next. But it would be simple enough to reduce a corpse to tiny pieces and feed it to the fish if that was what was required. "Easily done," he said.

The shipyard boss nodded and a slow smile spread across his face. "Then yeah, I think I might have just the job for you."

And so Lo Wang went to work for the labor union, conking heads and breaking kneecaps for a living. He had no papers, no fingerprints on file, no identity for the government regulators and investigators to pursue—he was the perfect man for the job. Wang didn't quite understand the hierarchy at first, but when he finally grasped it he was absolutely incredulous. He was working for the workers! The champion of the downtrodden, cleaning the system of those who tried to keep them from earning a decent wage.

Wang's own wage was paid under the table, tax free and never accounted for on any set of books, but Wang was proud to be part of the organization anyway. It was far more honest and upstanding than Zilla Enterprises had ever been.

Zilla. Wang had not forgotten his betrayal, and the cowardly way Zilla had tried to kill him after he had quit. Apparently Zilla had meant it when he said nobody left his employ alive. You had to be on his side or no one's side. Well, then, if he had chosen to make Lo Wang his enemy, then Wang would oblige him. He would gather his strength, prepare himself for battle, and return to Japan to seek revenge for the great wrong he had endured.

As long as he was in America, it made sense to learn American ways of fighting as well. Especially if he planned to go up against Zilla himself. That laser of his was a powerful weapon, faster than any of the traditional ninja's tools. Wang would need something similar if he hoped to win a direct confrontation. He could always try to sneak in and assassinate the Master in his sleep, but as a man of honor Wang preferred the forward approach. He would just make sure he was better armed than Zilla, that was all.

The other union muscle men were glad to show him their guns. They took Wang out to the shooting range, and once they explained to him how the weapons worked they were amazed at what he could do with them.

"Breathing, concentration, and muscle control,"

Wang instructed them. "And you must remember also, any projectile, even bullet, follows parabola described by equation vee sub eye times tee plus one half a times tee squared."

"How do you know all that stuff, anyway?" one of them asked him.

"I had good teacher," Wang replied. "Master Shoji taught me everything possible to know about fighting. Not with these weapons, but particles—no, sorry, principles are the same." He still had trouble with the language, but he didn't care. He didn't fight with words.

"Shee-it. Wish there was somebody like that around here."

Wang cocked the automatic weapon, a boxy thing of Austrian manufacture, and aimed at a row of beer bottles set on a rail just in front of the bullet deflection shield. Wang had laid them end on with their mouths facing him; now he set the selector for fully automatic fire and squeezed the trigger, carefully placing one bullet through the mouth of each bottle until he had knocked the bases out of them all without shattering the necks or the sides.

He looked over at his envious companions. "You wish for good teacher? Now you have one."

Chapter 7

Lo Wang's school achieved instant renown among the people who knew about that sort of thing. At first he taught only union enforcers, but as word spread he took on students from survivalist enclaves, independent businesses, and even the military's special forces.

He taught each of them the discipline and the fighting techniques of the ninja, and from each of them he learned whatever specialties they had. He learned about machine guns, shotguns, rocket launchers, flame throwers, and dozens of other high-tech weapons that he could use against Zilla.

When he judged that the time was right, he went back home to settle the score with his former employer, only to find that Zilla had vanished. His corporation still spread its tendrils into every aspect of the world economy it could reach, and Zilla was still on the road toward taking over Japan—and from there, the world—but all from behind carefully guarded secret identities. And no matter how hard he tried, Wang couldn't find the lead he needed to reach the heart of the organization.

The closest he came was in a little grocery near where he had first met Fuji. He heard a familiar voice and turned around to see Hiroyukia Nagano, one of his few friends from the early days with Zilla.

"Fuetsu!" he called out, for that was what he had called the man. It meant battle axe, and was meant as a compliment.

Fuetsu turned his head, puzzled.

"It's me, Lo Wang!"

Fuetsu's face went slack. All the blood drained away, leaving him pasty white.

Wang rushed to his aid. "What's the matter? Fuetsu!"

His old companion turned away. "You shouldn't be here," he said.

"I'm looking for Zilla," Wang told him.

"You don't want to find him. Go away. Go very far away."

"I've been in America," Wang said. "Now I'm back." In English, he said, "Tanned, rested, and ready."

Fuetsu didn't laugh. "Ready to die. You're a walking corpse already." He turned back to look at Wang. "And now so am I. Unless . . ."

"Unless what?"

Swift as a snake, Fuetsu struck out at Wang with his open palm, striking him on the side of the head. The blow would have killed him if Wang hadn't seen it coming at the last instant and moved with it. He jumped back to give himself room, but Fuetsu rushed him, picking up a lemon from a bin on the way and hurling it at Wang's eyes.

"Stop!" Wang said, batting it aside. It sprayed pulp across a window, and the rind hit so hard it cracked the glass. "I don't want to fight you."

"Then stand still and let me kill you. If I give Zilla your head, maybe he will let me live."

"You know where he is?" Wang asked.

"No, but he knows where I am."

Fuetsu pulled an aikuchi from a wrist sheath and flung the knife at Wang's chest. Wang knocked that aside, too, careful to direct it into a coconut where it wouldn't hurt anyone.

Fuetsu could see that he was outclassed. In a last desperate attempt he rushed directly at Wang, throwing lemons and oranges and apples at him to keep him busy until he drew close enough to pull out his sword and bring it down in a fast arc toward Wang's head.

Wang had trained his own reflexes as well as those of his American students. When he saw the sword rise, his right hand moved of its own volition to the sawed-off shotgun at his side, drew it, and pulled the trigger. Buckshot tore open Fuetsu's chest the moment his sword started to descend, blasting him backward into a bin of oranges, which cascaded to the floor around his twitching body. His sword clattered to the floor as well.

Wang bent down next to his fallen comrade. "I am sorry, but you left me no choice."

Excited voices reminded him where he was. He had been so focused on Fuetsu, and on finding Zilla, that he had forgotten. Now he looked up and saw a sea of faces, mouths open in wide Os of surprise, staring at him.

Sirens blared a few blocks away. Someone had alerted the police. Wang stood up. The onlookers parted, giving him a clear path out of the grocery. He looked back at Fuetsu's body, then shook his head sadly. He had had no idea how badly Zilla wanted him dead.

He tucked the shotgun back into the folds of his clothing, then stepped out into the crowd. The people in front shied away from him, but within a few steps he had gone beyond the ones who had actually witnessed the fight. He heard cries of "There, that's him!" and "Who, that one?" but he ignored them all. Half the trick to vanishing in plain sight was to simply become part of the scenery. By the time he reached the end of the block and turned the corner, he had become just another person in the crowd.

That was the easiest of his brushes with Zilla. Every time he made contact after that, no matter how brief or insignificant, the reprisal was instantaneous. Word had gotten out that he was there, so it was no longer just one on one, either. Legions of ninja would swarm out of nowhere, and when Zilla ran out of ninja he switched to his hellish dark phantoms. If Wang hadn't been armed to the teeth with high-tech hardware he wouldn't have survived the first day, but he stuck it out for over a month before he backed off to rethink his strategy. He couldn't keep up a direct assault; he needed to find someone who knew Zilla's whereabouts, capture them, and torture the information out of them.

Trouble was, Zilla's business associates in Japan

were on the alert now, and too well guarded. Wang
was going to have to find his contact somewhere else.
Somewhere like America, where Zilla Enterprises was
starting to spread its tentacles as well.

So it was back to the U.S., this time to New York,
the international business hub of the world. Wang's
luck changed for the better there; from a Zilla associate in a sushi bar he got half of a name of someone
who could take him to his leader. "Tanaka," the man
had told him in exchange for a quick death. The name
was practically useless, as it was one of the most
common names in Japan, but it was all Wang had to
go on.

And then a man named Jefferson Adams had come
calling. He was from the CIA, and he had a problem.
Someone had stolen a top secret device, code named
the ABCD device, from a private laboratory and the
CIA wanted it back. In return for Wang's help, Adams
would give Wang Tanaka's first name, which the CIA
had just recently learned in their own investigation of
Zilla's expanding empire.

It was the best deal Wang was liable to get. Adams
was crazy, of course—he claimed that the ABCD
device could be used to start and stop earthquakes—
but Wang humored him so he could learn the name.
When the planet-wide rattling started a few days later,
Wang realized Adams had been telling the truth. In
fact the situation was worse than Adams had revealed. It was in all the newscasts: ABCD stood for
Artificial Beginning of Continental Drift. Someone
was using the device to move all the continents
together, to re-create Pangaea.

The trail of the ABCD device had led from New

York to France. On the plane Wang had met a woman named Florelle, who said she was the daughter of Dr. Morgan, the inventor of the device, who had been kidnapped along with it. Florelle wanted to join forces with Wang, and although he preferred to work alone, he couldn't deny her right to rescue her mother. Besides, she had such soft, olive skin, long blond hair, and high, firm breasts that strained the confines of her blouse. Wang had always had trouble when he let his little brain overrule his big brain, but it spoke with authority this time. So they had gone to France together, and traced a lead from there to Spain, where Wang had been sure he'd found the operation's secret headquarters in a huge underground cavern. . . .

Chapter 8

. . . The very cavern in which he now lay underneath a pile of rubble, victim of an ingenious trap sprung by the mastermind of the whole ABCD affair, Dr. Exo.

It was so embarrassing. Wang had never even gotten close to Exo. He knew nothing about the man; Exo was just a name given to him by a man named Adams. Wang had been running around Europe with a beautiful woman while Exo had been shaking the Earth to its very foundations, and what had Wang done to stop it? Wang, the great hope of the civilized world, the only man skilled enough to enter Exo's evil lair and stop his infernal plan? Well, he had killed several beast men, of which there were probably thousands more just like them. He had stopped an airline hijacking. He had set a record for the shortest time across the English Channel on foot, without even walking on water.

And what else? Wang racked his brain for anything

more that could put a positive spin on his last moments of life, but the in-flight movie had run out. He had failed, and because of his weakness the entire planet was doomed.

Even now he could feel the vibration in the Earth as the continents slid toward one another. Europe wasn't moving much compared to the others, but ripples from earthquakes all across the world still shook the ground. Eventually, Wang knew, they would shake the boulders under which he was trapped into a compact pile, with Wang no more than a thin layer at the bottom.

The blood from the beast men had pooled beneath him now, covering the rocky cavern floor. His own blood flowed freely from countless wounds. It coated his entire body. Even his sumo tuft on the back of his head, and the long Fu Manchu beard on his chin, were soaked. He must look a sight, he thought, if there had been light enough to see by or anyone left alive to see him. He wondered if there was anyone in the cavern to even hear his last words, whatever those might be. Should he go for one last expression of defiance, or something more cryptic, like the last words of Master Shoji?

And then it hit him. Shoji's dying words. Not a self-aggrandizing pronouncement or a rant against cruel fate, but an attempt to impart just one more piece of information that his student might find useful in a tight situation.

A situation like this one, in fact. Pinned under a mountain of rubble, the rough limestone surfaces of freshly broken boulders holding him as effectively as a thousand clinging hands.

How had Shoji put it? "Remember, the coefficient of friction is dependent upon two things: the nature of the surface and . . ."

And the force pressing them together. Wang couldn't do much about that, but the nature of the surface was changing with every drop of slippery blood that flowed over the rock and over Wang's own rough skin.

"Hah!" he shouted, momentarily overcoming the weight of the boulders on his chest in his excitement. "The blood of my enemies shall be my salvation!"

He wiggled left and right, spreading the blood around, then breathed out every last molecule of air from his lungs. He flattened his body as far as it would go, then pushed with his feet and pulled with his free hand against the boulders that trapped him.

Pain lanced through him as sharp rock edges cut into his chest and back, but he slid forward an inch. "Pain is for the weak," he told himself, and he pushed again. More motion—until his weapons belt hung up on an edge. In the tight confines he couldn't get his hands down to unfasten it, so he continued to push, hoping the force wouldn't shift the boulders and bring them down the last few inches it would take to crush him.

The one at his feet shifted, and a terrible grinding screech of sliding rock came from just overhead. This was it. Wang kicked and pulled with all his strength, and just as the slab of rock above him started to move, his belt snapped.

Wang shot out of the crevice like a cork out of a champagne bottle, and his trajectory ended in the same fashion. Fortunately the boulder his head smacked against was angled, and he only left a patch of skin behind as he bounced off it.

He wasn't free yet. The entire cavern shook with the rumble of shifting boulders. It was pitch black, and Wang didn't know where the exit—or even a safe pocket—was. He waved his arms around before him, feeling for a passage, a flat wall he could take shelter against, anything. All he felt was jagged rock.

The noise sounded different off to his left. Wang turned, listening. Yes, the echoes were stronger from that direction. That might mean it was simply deeper in the cavern, but it definitely meant that there was more open space, and right now open space was what he needed most. Wang scrambled through the shifting boulders, climbing upward wherever he could, and eventually reached the top of the rubble heap.

He blinked in amazement. There was light. It was only a dim glow from a single red LED on some piece of battery-powered machinery on a far wall, but it was light. Light enough to see the jumbled hulks of rock that littered the cavern. Light enough to see the vast open space that remained overhead, where Exo's bomb had only carved out another, higher ceiling to the vast underground chamber.

And light enough to see the three genetically altered beast men who waited for him by the boulder-choked entrance. One of whom held Florelle's unconscious body in its arms.

Wang instinctively reached for his Uzis, but they were somewhere under the rubble. So were his riot gun, his missile launcher, his sword, and all the other weapons he normally carried. Even his shuriken had been attached to his weapons belt.

It looked like a bare-hands fight, three to one, mano a mano, with Flo as the prize. Wang clenched and unclenched his fists, working the kinks out of his fingers. Every one of them would have to be a lethal weapon now.

The air was still full of rock dust from the explosion, but he took a deep breath, then advanced toward the three beasts.

"Who—goes—there?" one asked in a slow, growly voice, squinting into the darkness. He apparently didn't see very well; that meant he wasn't a tiger-man, at least.

There was no honor in trickery. Wang bellowed at the top of his lungs, "I am Lo Wang, Shadow Warrior! The darkness made man, the night made flesh. Nothing shall stand in my way!"

The humanoid who had spoken looked to the others, then all three burst out laughing. From the sounds of it they were a bear-man, a hyena-man, and an ape-man.

That was not the response Wang had expected. Warily, he advanced to within a few yards of them and saw what had made them laugh: the cavern entrance beside them was packed solid with boulders the size of cars that had been shoved there by the force of the blast.

"You are trapped," Wang said.

"So are you, hahahaha!" said the hyena hybrid in a fast, high voice.

He wouldn't be if he could find his weapons. A few

well-placed sticky bombs would loosen that rock jam. But all his weapons were underneath even more debris than what blocked the doorway, and Wang wasn't going back under there after them.

He jumped to another boulder within arms' reach of the beast men, ready to kill them all with his bare hands if they even twitched wrong. They all shifted warily, nervously fingering their weapons, which they unfortunately hadn't lost in the explosion, but they waited to see what he would do. Apparently if all of them were trapped they didn't see any point in continuing their fight.

"How bad she hurt?" Wang asked the one who held Flo.

It was the ape-man. She lay on her back in his hairy arms, her head lolled backward and one arm dangling loosely, her breasts slowly rising and falling with each breath. In the red glow from the cavern's single light, she looked unearthly pale. Glistening trickles of moisture ran along her arms and across her face. It took Wang a moment to realize it was blood; in the red light it was the same color as her skin. The ape-man looked down at her face, then back at Wang. "She bleeds. She breathes. She needs."

What she needed was a good doctor. Wang considered rescuing her from the ape-man, but the tender way the creature held her made him pause. The ape-man was obviously smitten by her beauty. He wasn't going to hurt her, at least not right away, and she probably *would* be injured in a fight, so it made sense to leave her in his arms for now.

"Is this only way out of here?" Wang asked.

"It isn't a way out," said the hyena-man. "No way out, no way, no place."

"Have you even tried?" Wang jumped from boulder to boulder around the three mutants, ready at any moment to defend himself if they moved against him, but they let him go. He climbed up the pile of debris, examining the way the rocks rested against each other. It looked like the ejecta from the explosion had rushed into the cave mouth and met more ejecta from a separate explosion there; that was the only scenario that would explain the way the boulders were piled all the way to the ceiling. There wasn't even a gap big enough for a bloody arm to squeeze through, much less a whole person.

Wang climbed back down the slanted pile of rubble and examined the boulders at its base. If one of them were to slide backward, the rest would lose their support and the whole pile might shift, maybe leaving a gap at the top.

Might. Maybe. But it was all he had to go on. He pushed at the most obvious one, a rectangular slab the size of a grand piano, but it didn't budge. Nor did any of the others he put his weight behind. Some blood might help, but Wang wasn't dripping enough to matter now, and all the corpses were under the big rock pile in the middle of the cavern. Somehow he didn't suppose the beast men would voluntarily give up any of their own, either.

"We have tried pushing," rumbled the bear-man. "All three of us together. It is no use."

"So what is plan?" Wang asked, standing up and relaxing his tight muscles. "Just wait here to die? Eat one another until we run out of food?"

"You're the hu-man," said the ape-man. "You tell us."

These creatures had obviously been bred for fighting, not for thinking. They'd probably even been bred for subservience to true men. They were willing to take orders from the same guy they had been fighting only a few minutes earlier. Wang looked them over: the big, hulking bear-man had to weigh at least five hundred pounds. The hyena-man was wiry and light, but all muscle, and the ape-man's long arms had more leverage than Wang's legs.

"Three of you not enough, eh?" Wang asked. "Then we try four. You," he said, pointing to the ape-man, "take Flo back along side of cavern and put her down somewhere safe, then come back and help."

The ape-man did as he asked. Wang and the others eyed each other silently, sizing each other up, until he returned. When they were all four present again, Wang moved into a position where he could push with his shoulder and hands against the piano-sized boulder and brace his feet against a boulder behind it. The others moved in next to him, and he repressed a shudder as the bear-man's hairy chest pressed against his back and his hot, sour breath blew on his neck. This was definitely too close for comfort. But all three beast men merely tested their grip and waited for the signal to push.

"Remember," Wang told them, "once it start moving, keep pushing. Sliding friction is always less than static friction."

The hyena-man looked at him uncomprehendingly, and Wang knew now how Master Shoji had felt all those years ago. "Never mind," he said. "Just push until I tell you stop."

Wang took a moment to focus his chi energy, directing the earth force through every muscle, making each one as strong as steel. His entire body became a coiled spring ready to explode into action.

"Ready . . . set . . . shove!" Wang said, and he uncoiled.

Rock grains pressed deep into his shoulder and hands. The beast men grunted with effort. Wang heard the boulder screech under the new stress, but it only moved a fraction of an inch.

"I . . . am . . . Lo Wang!" he shouted. "Shadow Warrior. The darkness made man, the night made flesh. Nothing shall stand in my way!" He summoned every last erg of energy he could produce and poured it all into the rock.

His speech seemed to galvanize the others as well. The bear-man grunted and lowered his head, the hyena-man barked, and the ape-man howled a blood-curdling yell. All four pushed for all they were worth.

The boulder shifted. Rock ground against rock. A deep rumble filled the cavern, and suddenly the resistance eased off as the boulder began to slide.

"Push!" Wang yelled, taking one step, then another to keep up with the moving chunk of stone.

The rumbling grew louder, and suddenly Wang realized the flaw in his plan. He was between a rock that had held back an entire slope and the slope itself. "Get clear!" he shouted, scrambling for the top of the boulder. The ape-man was right behind him, and the bear-man lumbered away sideways, but the hyena-man slipped while trying to climb the rock face and nearly fell under the advancing slope before Wang reached down and grabbed his arm and dragged him to safety.

The three of them rode the rectangular boulder like surfers on a wave until it slammed up against another one and pitched them off. Wang leaped to another and another beyond that, one step ahead of the rock slide, until the deafening roar of shifting rock died down.

He looked back. The hyena-man was right behind him, but the ape-man was nowhere to be seen. He had apparently slipped and been crushed beneath the boulders.

A shaft of white light from the cavern mouth lit up the dusty air. "Free!" the hyena-man yelled. "Free, free, free!" He scrambled up the boulders, momentarily blotting out the light, and disappeared. Wang could hear him clattering down the other side, still shouting, "Free, free, free!"

The bear-man stood alongside the cavern wall, watching Wang. Wang jumped from boulder to boulder, giving him wide berth, until he found where the ape-man had laid Flo. She was still unconscious, but breathing steadily. Wang picked her up and draped her over his shoulder, and as he did so he slipped her little .38 out from its holster, just in case. He held it close to her hip, out of sight as he turned around with her.

His instincts were still good. The bear-man had his weapon drawn, a tubular electromagnetic rail gun, aimed right at Wang.

"That very bad idea," Wang told him.

"Voices in . . . head," the bear-man growled. "I must . . . kill."

Wang emptied the .38 into him, choosing his targets carefully. Normally a .38 would do nothing against a bear, but this was a bear-man hybrid. Wang went for the soft spots just the same, shooting him between the ribs, in the eyes, and when the bear-man jerked sideways, in the ear. The already-dead beast's twitching fingers fired one shot into the ceiling, knocking down a spray of rock, then he crashed to the floor of the cavern.

Voices in his head? Radio-control? Wang wondered. It had to be. The transmitter in the cave had evidently been destroyed in the blast, leaving the beast men free to think on their own, but once there was an open path to the surface, a signal from outside had been able to penetrate to the bear-man.

Then the hyena-man would be waiting outside. Wang set Flo down by the dead bear-man, picked up his rail gun, and climbed carefully up the rock slope.

No shots greeted him. Wang ripped off a shred of his pants leg and waved it in the opening at the top. Nothing. He stuck his head up for a quick glimpse, then dropped down into cover again, but nothing happened. The image that had flashed onto his retinae held no hyena-man.

Wang took a longer look, and then he spotted the mutant warrior running away through the brushy landscape outside the cave for all he was worth. That was even worse than an ambush, Wang realized. If the hyena-man got away, then Exo would know that Wang had survived.

He aimed the rail gun and pulled the trigger. With a loud hum, a pulse of electricity flung a steel slug at high velocity out into the plain. A puff of dirt exploded beside the hyena-man. There must have been wind outside blowing the shots sideways. Wang aimed into the wind and sqeezed the trigger again, but nothing happened. The rail gun was empty.

Chapter 9

The hotel was small and anonymous, one of hundreds like it in all the small tourist towns of southern Spain. Adobe walls, red tile roofs, an enclosed courtyard where guests met at night to drink and eat and party.

Wang and Flo didn't party. The other guests in the hotel—the few who hadn't fled for home the moment the continents had begun to move—didn't even know they were there. The manager himself didn't know about Wang; he had rented the room to a disheveled American woman who explained that she had gotten mad at her husband after a fight and ditched him in Cádiz, and she didn't want to be bothered by anyone, not even the housekeepers. Wang had slipped in at dusk, cloaking himself in shadow and using his ninja skills of blending in with the background to make him nearly invisible as he slid down the hallway and into the room where Flo waited.

She had not been hurt as badly as he had feared.

The blood on her arms and face had proved to be someone else's, he discovered when he stopped at a stream not far outside the cave and dribbled cold water over her forehead. She was bruised and exhausted, but otherwise unharmed. Wang was amazed by her resilience; her bones seemed more supple than any Wang had ever seen before. And she had the endurance of any ninja. After she had awakened at the stream she had soaked her feet in the cool water for a few minutes, growing visibly stronger by the second, then she had put her shoes back on and suggested that they hide out at a hotel while they gathered the rest of their strength.

There was only one bed. Neither minded, but neither had the strength to take advantage of the situation, either. By the time they arrived at the hotel they didn't even have the strength to take off their clothing. Wang helped Flo lie back with her head on a pillow and a damp cloth on her forehead, then he lay beside her on his back and prepared to enter a deep yoga trance while his body slowly healed itself of all the knocks and cuts he had received.

He could still feel the vibration transmitted through the ground from the earthquakes elsewhere in the world. By morning, all the pieces in the Pangaea puzzle would be hundreds of miles closer together. Wang sighed. He couldn't stop it tonight. He didn't even know where Exo's actual headquarters was. The cave had been nothing more than a trap; Exo could be calling the shots from anywhere in the world.

Tomorrow. Wang would save what was left of the world tomorrow, but tonight he had to regain his strength.

Just as he was about to drift into oblivion, he heard someone scratching at the wall in the bathroom. Then came a muffled thump. He rose up to listen, but the sound stopped in the same instant. It had sounded exactly like someone brushing against a wall and then thumping it, feeling for a weak spot that they could kick their way through.

Had Exo found them already? It seemed unlikely. If Exo knew they were here he would have destroyed the hotel, maybe even the entire town, not sent a single assassin to finish them off.

Zilla? Equally unlikely, for the same reason.

Who was it then? Wang got up and waited in the bathroom doorway, crouched in the stance that would let him attack instantly if someone were to come through the wall.

The hotel had been built for tourists. It wasn't like the older ones that had been retrofitted for plumbing, with the pipes bolted to stone walls; this one had the pipes built in. There was a sink just to the left of the doorway, a light blue porcelain toilet straight ahead, and a bathtub and shower to the right. A fluorescent light flickered annoyingly overhead.

Nobody came through the wall. Wang listened for any hint of activity in the room on the other side, but all was silent. After five minutes of nothing, Wang decided it must have been the building settling, or a rat inside the wall. He went back to the bed and lay back down.

He was halfway through his relaxation routine when the sound came again. The same brushing, then a thump. Wang rolled to his feet and took up position in the bathroom doorway again, vowing to wait this time until he knew for sure what had caused the noise.

It was a long wait. Sixteen minutes, thirty-five seconds by his count. But then it came again, and Wang's ears zeroed in directly on the source: the toilet's fill valve had turned on, water had flowed for just a second, then the toilet had shut off. Wonderful. It must have a leaky tank, and one of those instant-on-instant-off valves. Wang nearly laughed at his paranoia, but he didn't. It wasn't paranoia when people really were out to get you.

He couldn't sleep with this going on every sixteen minutes. Oh, he could—a Shadow Warrior learned to control his hearing as well as the rest of his body—but if he tuned out the plumbing and then somebody *did* try to break in, he would lose the first crucial seconds of warning before they came through the walls.

He looked below the water tank. No shut-off valve. Of course not; this was a tourist hotel, and tourists were too stupid and vandalism prone to trust with something like that out in the open. All the service lines to the toilet and the sink and the shower were hidden inside the wall.

Wang sighed. There was nothing else he could do; he closed the bathroom door so the noise wouldn't disturb Flo, then he bent down beside the toilet and jabbed quickly with his fingers extended into the wall. Kay equals one half em vee squared; move fast enough and there's practically no resistance to wallboard, and practically no noise. He punched a rough rectangle into the wall where he hoped the pipes were, pried the chalky board loose, and peered into the hole.

No pipes. They were evidently on the other side of the tank. Wang shifted over and tried that side, but he was too low, so he had to try again a little higher before he found the water line. There was no shut-off valve inside the wall, either, but the pipe was soft copper, so Wang gripped it in his hand and squeezed, flattening it and kinking it until no water could flow through it.

He backed off and waited. Sixteen minutes, seventeen, eighteen . . . No noise. Good. Now he could sleep.

He thought no more of it until he heard Flo get up in the middle of the night, heard her flip on the bathroom light, and scream.

"What?" he asked, coming fully awake in an instant and leaping up off the bed to go to her aid.

"Somebody broke in!" she whispered, backing away from the open doorway. "They—I don't get it. Is this some kind of bizarre warning?"

Wang looked into the bathroom just to make sure what she was talking about. It was just as he had left it: holes in the wall, shards of wallboard on the floor. "No," he told her. "I did that."

She looked at him with her head tilted slightly sideways. "Why?"

"Because it—well, because—long story," said Wang, struggling for words. "Here, I turn water back on for you." He reached into the hole he had gouged in the wall and uncrimped the pipe, careful not to flex it too far and burst it. The toilet began to fill.

"Are you going to have to do that every time I want to pee?" she asked incredulously.

"If Wang wants sleep, yes."

She looked at him again, then shook her head. "I knew there was something strange about you the moment we met."

"You were one who wanted to follow me," Wang reminded her.

"So I did." She stepped into the bathroom and closed the door. Wang went back to the bed and lay down again. There was something strange about her, too, something besides her love of water and her peculiar way of flirting with him by questioning everything he said or did, but he still couldn't put his finger on it. In time, he told himself. All things will become clear in time.

When she finished in the bathroom, Wang went back in and crimped the water pipe again. When he crouched down beside the stool to do so, he noticed wet footprints on the floor; small ones from bare feet. Flo's shoes lay beside the bathtub, and the bottom of the tub was wet as well. She had been soaking her feet again. He shrugged, turned off the light, and went back to bed.

He woke to the sound of birds just outside his window, and when he opened his eyes he saw that the sun was already up and peeking through the slats in the blinds. Another day, another horde of mutant beast men to vanquish.

Flo was still asleep. Wang watched her for a moment, enjoying the sight of her soft skin in the early morning light. She looked more like a statue than a person. She hardly even breathed. Wang had never seen someone truly sleep like a log before, but Flo had the form down perfectly.

Let her rest. He got up and uncrimped the water

pipe again and got ready to shower. He had just turned on the hot water and was stepping into the tub when there was a soft knock on the door and Flo opened it. "Need someone to wash your back?" she asked.

She was already undressed. Wang looked her up and down appraisingly. Her wavy blond hair cascaded down around her shoulders, stopping just short of her high, round breasts. She had an hourglass figure, and her legs tapered gracefully down to delicate feet. Her olive skin had just a faint hint of green to it in the fluorescent light.

"You would like to wash Wang?" he asked, just to make sure he understood her correctly.

"That's the general idea," she replied, grinning. "I thought maybe I could thank you properly for saving my life."

"That not required," Wang told her, "but come shower anyway, if you like."

She looked him over just as appraisingly as he had her. "I think I like. They don't call you Lo Wang for nothing, do they?" She stepped into the shower with him, took the soap, and began rubbing it over his chest.

"Mmm, I drop soap, you bend over, pick it up," he said playfully.

She laughed. "Why, look. Should I call you Hi Wang now?"

"You can call Wang whatever you like," he said, taking the soap from her and caressing her delicate body with his rough hands. "That is, if you can find breath to speak." He reached out and turned up the heat. A little while later when the water began to cool, he turned that up, too.

They were just toweling off when there was a knock on the door. Wang and Flo exchanged a glance, then Wang dropped his towel on the dresser and moved silently over to stand by the door. He nodded slowly to Flo, and she called out, "Who is it?"

"Jefferson Adams," a familiar voice replied. Wang turned the doorknob, but didn't pull open the door. When Adams pushed it open himself, Wang grabbed his arm the moment it cleared the jamb and yanked him into the room, whirled him around with his arm behind his back, and wrapped his own arm around the CIA man's neck.

Adams was a nondescript government man with a face his own mother would have trouble spotting in a crowd of two. The generic man behind the counter, with his round face and beady brown eyes and cheap brown suit. He normally wore a smarmy smile that made Wang feel like washing, but he wasn't smiling now.

"Nice to see you, too," Adams croaked out.

"You sent us into trap," Wang told him, nudging the door shut with his foot and pulling Adams away from it.

"Exo sent you into a trap," Adams replied. "He intercepted Dr. Morgan's emergency beacon transmission and substituted his own coordinates. We've got the real thing now."

"Mother?" Flo asked. "Where is she?"

Adams looked over at her, standing there beside the

bed with just a towel wrapped around her. Wang didn't have even that much on, but Adams couldn't see that from the position he was in. Still, it wouldn't take a genius to figure out what they'd been doing.

"Looks like you're getting along nicely these days," he said. "Did the Earth move last night for you, too?"

Flo glared. "Where's my mother?" she asked again, with exaggerated patience.

"Australia," Adams said quickly. "Ayers Rock."

"What's Ayers Rock?"

"A big rock in the middle of the outback with a whole lot of nothing around it. But underneath it is apparently the nerve complex for Exo's entire operation."

"I don't like underground places," Wang said. "The last one fell in on me."

"So wear a hard hat." Adams tugged at Wang's arm, and Wang let him go. Adams massaged his neck and his kinked arm, saying, "Look, you're our only hope of getting in there and you know it. And if you think the earthquakes were bad when the accelerated continental drift started, just wait until the continents start slamming into one another at a couple hundred miles an hour. Nine tenths of the world's population is going to die in the first day, and the rest will probably kill each other off fighting for food before things settle down enough to grow anything more. You want to try your luck in that kind of world, stick around here and play body games with each other. You don't have to go looking for trouble; it'll come to you soon enough."

"I want to find my mother," Flo said.

"I want to find Zilla and stick head on spike," Wang

said. "I have already learned name of his contact man. If Lo Wang does this for you, what else can you offer?"

"Not a damn thing," Adams told him. "You can do it for the sake of humanity or not at all. Your choice."

Wang picked up his towel from the dresser and finished drying off. "I want name now, in case you die in days to come."

"After you've stopped Exo and retrieved the ABCD device," Adams said. "That was our agreement."

Wang considered extracting the information from the CIA agent by torture. He suspected he could make him sing it to the tune of the "Star Spangled Banner" within five minutes if he wanted to, but that would ruin his usefulness as an information source after that. No, Wang wouldn't know until he tried to use the name to track down Zilla whether it would be enough, and if it wasn't, then it might be necessary to tap into the CIA's spy network again for more clues.

Adams was waiting for an answer.

Wang picked up his bloodstained black pants and pulled them on. "I need weapons," he said at last.

Chapter 10

Adams had arranged a military flight for them, but Wang had a bad feeling about trusting him that far. He gave Adams the slip as soon as he had restocked his personal arsenal.

That had been so simple to do it was pathetic. On the way out of the El Cid Armas y Quincalleria, laden with an enormous camouflage duffel bag full of goodies, Wang made a big show of holding open the heavy metal security door for Flo. He then stepped outside himself, shut the door in the surprised Adams's face, and pushed back on it, wedging the tang of the lock tight against the strike plate. Adams tried turning the knob, but there was too much force holding it fast. Wang dug into his pocket for a couple of pesetas and wedged them into the crack between the door and the jamb so they would keep the pressure on the latch.

"What are you doing?" Adams demanded. "Open the door!"

"Ancient Japanese saying," Wang replied. "The coefficient of friction depends upon two things: nature of surface, and force pressing them together."

"That's not ancient," Flo said. "And it's not Japanese, either."

"Tell that to Master Shoji," Wang said. "He was very old when he say that. Old as man can be. And definitely Japanese." He picked up his duffel bag and urged Flo out to Adams's car, which waited by the curb.

"You don't have the keys," she reminded him as she climbed in. Inside the shop they could hear Adams cursing in English and the shop owner saying something to him in Spanish.

"Keys are for the meek," Wang said. He threw his duffel bag in the back seat, climbed into the driver's seat, reached under the dashboard beside the steering column and yanked out a fistful of wires, which he began shorting out one by one. The lights flashed on, the wipers swept across the windshield, the horn blared—and then the engine started.

He shoved the car into gear and gunned it down the street just as a loud explosion from behind them blew the shop door outward onto the sidewalk. Adams and the shop owner rushed out, waving away the smoke, but Wang screeched around the corner at the end of the block and they were gone from sight.

"Where are we going?" Flo asked him, buckling her seatbelt as he sped through the narrow Spanish streets. Cars honked at him and he veered toward them like a local driver would, forcing them off the road at the last minute.

"The airport," he replied.

"You plan to just walk up to the counter and buy a couple of tickets to Australia? Heathrow was a ghost town when we flew in yesterday. What makes you think there'll be anyone flying today?"

"Another ancient Japanese saying," Wang said. "Pay high, rickshaw fly. You still have credit card, yes?"

"Yeah, but if nobody's at the ticket counter, what good will it—"

"Millions of tourists stranded in quakes," Wang said. "Rich, whiney tourists. Call embassies, wave green pictures of dead presidents. Planes fly today." He shifted down to swerve around a young woman on a bicycle. "So yes, you walk up to counter and buy tickets to Australia. I will make separate way to gate where flight departs while you do that."

"Why?"

"Because I think Wang probably have trouble walking through security checkpoint with bag full of guns."

"Oh," she said. Then, "Can't you just check it at the ticket counter?"

"I want it with me on flight."

"Why?"

"Call it insurance."

"Insurance against what? If you use one of those macho man's testosterone boosters inside a plane, we're all going to be toast."

"I hope leaving Adams out of plans make less danger of that," Wang told her, "but I like to keep options open. Is possible Exo might learn where we are even though Adams not know."

Flo shuddered.

"Are you sure you want to come with Lo Wang?" he asked her.

She smiled briefly and leaned up against him. "Lo Wang, Hi Wang, I'll follow you anywhere. You know that."

"You think with little brain," he told her.

"And you don't?"

"Of course I do, but both *my* brains trained for battle."

"That's something I'd like to see. You fighting off an attacker with your 'little brain.'"

Wang leered at her. "Little brain has caused little death for many women." Then he lost his smile. "If you come with me, Exo could cause big death for you. Not nearly as fun."

"Look," she said. "He kidnapped my mother. It's her device that's moving the continents around. I've got to help."

"All right," Wang said. "But don't complain if you get killed. This not be as easy as it was in cave."

When they reached the airport he let Flo out at the terminal building, then drove on around to the employees' parking lot and parked the car. The airport was busy with people desperate to get home in the midst of the world crisis, and there were cars double parked everywhere, but Wang cruised the lot until he found an empty spot and parked properly. Even so he took all the identification papers out of the glove box, got his bag out of the back seat, locked the car, then ripped loose the license plates and tossed the papers and plates in a garbage can. It would be a long time before anyone could trace the car to Adams, much less to Wang and Flo. By then they would already be in Australia.

He sauntered over to the entrance, swinging his bag back and forth and whistling softly. The door had an electronic security lock, which meant there was no live guard. Good. Wang waited for the proper moment, then gave the bag a boost on the upswing and tossed it onto the flat roof. It landed with a muffled clang. Two more steps and he leaped upward himself, caught the edge of the roof, and pulled himself up.

The roof was dotted with vent stacks and air conditioning units. Wang walked among them toward the other side of the building, to the point where three concourses split off and reached their long fingers out into the concrete parking apron. He looked at the airplanes for clues, saw a 747 with a big kangaroo on the tail, and smiled. Quantas. Never a crash.

Then he noticed movement on the roof of the next concourse over, the one where El Al and Pan Am and Aeroflot parked, and he lost his smile. Someone had just ducked behind an air vent.

There was no simpler way to look like you were sneaking around than to sneak around, especially if nobody was looking for you yet. That was such a basic rule that Wang could hardly believe his eyes, but a few seconds later another figure darted out from a different air vent and sprinted the few yards to another. It looked like a man in a black jogging suit with a white towel wrapped around his head.

A third figure made the crossing. They were heading out toward the planes. The last one carried a small duffel bag that looked like it held something heavy.

Wang paused at the juncture between concourses. It

was really none of his business, but he knew those three were up to no good. They had probably decided to take advantage of the confusion and make some kind of idiotic political "statement" involving bombs.

Wang had seen the results of other such statements. The people who made them showed no class. They didn't discriminate between the innocent and the guilty; they just wanted to kill people to get attention. A proper statement meant picking a specific target, a person who deserved making an example of, and then mailing his associates his head in a box. Or cooking his private parts over a brazier and eating them in front of the people who needed to witness it; Wang had found that equally effective. But bombing an airplane? It was an offense to the underworld.

Wang walked casually over to the nearest air conditioner and squatted down behind it. He opened his bag and pulled out a new weapons belt, filled it with shuriken and sticky bombs and ammunition, then strapped on his dual Uzis and hefted his riot gun in his hand. It was all overkill, but he liked being prepared. Just for familiarity he strapped on his sword as well, then he advanced up the roof of the concourse in silent, almost instantaneous jumps from one item of cover to the next. This was how you *sneaked*.

The terrorists never saw him coming. The one in back, the one carrying the bag with the bomb in it, was waiting for a signal to advance when Wang tapped him on the shoulder. He flinched so hard that he might have toppled off the roof if Wang hadn't caught him by the neck and pulled him back behind the cylindrical air vent he was hiding in the shadow of. Then he lunged for a .45 auto at his hip, but Wang reached down and broke his fingers. He had to squeeze the terrorist's neck with the other hand to keep him from screaming.

The guy was determined, Wang would give him that. He tried to cross-draw the .45 with his other hand, and Wang had to break that too, and then he tried kicking Wang in the crotch with his boots. A moment later he had two broken arms and two broken legs, and Wang still had not let him utter a sound.

"Let's see what's in bag," Wang said softly, using his free hand to rip open the heavy nylon. Sure enough, it was a bomb. A crude one, just a foot long section of two-inch-diameter pipe filled with plastique or some such, capped on both ends and with a timer taped to the middle. Crude, and not nearly big enough to harm a building much, but it would probably blow a hole in the side of an airplane. In flight, that could be deadly.

"Naughty, naughty," Wang said, shaking his head. "As if people don't have enough trouble in lives already. What is Wang to do with you?" He turned the terrorist's head around so he faced Wang, but didn't let go of his windpipe to let him speak. "That was rhetorical question," Wang informed him when he began to struggle again. "Hmm. I have to think on this a while. Hope you don't mind waiting few minutes to die." Wang unwound the towel from the terrorist's head, tore a thick strip off it with his teeth, and used that to gag him. Then he tied all four broken appendages together with the rest of the towel and left' him there with his bomb while he stalked the others.

They were looking back for their companion, so it wasn't as easy to sneak up on them. Wang had to use every trick he knew: sliding along in shadows, unscrewing a nut from a piece of sheet metal and tossing it ahead for a moment's distraction, reflecting sunlight into their eyes to blind them. He even called upon the mysterious *ku*, the power of the void, to cloak him in shadow while in the open. Eventually he crept up to an air conditioning unit only a few yards away from the one that the second terrorist hid in the shadow of. Wang knew that the man was looking backwards toward his missing companion; he waited patiently until he saw a shadow sliding along the roof toward him.

A machine pistol appeared first, followed by the second terrorist, come to investigate his companion's disappearance. He wasn't expecting anything this close. It took him a moment to register Wang's presence, and by then he was directly alongside him. Wang snatched his gun away before he could fire it, then pulled him into cover and disabled him the same way he had the first.

He pulled the turban off his captive's head and stuck it on his own, then peeked up over the air conditioner. The first terrorist was looking back toward him. He evidently had eyes good enough to recognize Wang's as the wrong ones under the turban, or else he had seen his companion's involuntary sideways lurch, but whatever the tipoff, Wang saw the muzzle flash of an automatic rifle and heard bullets ricochet off the air conditioner. Some of them punched through the radiator and refrigerant started boiling off into the air. Wang ducked down behind the compressor and quickly bared his second captive's right arm, cut it with his aikuchi until blood flowed freely, then flopped it out from behind the air conditioner. With luck the lead terrorist would think he had killed Wang rather than his own man, but either way he would have to come back and see.

Wang waited, listening for clues, but the air conditioner drowned out any noise. He looked for telltale shadows, but there were none. This terrorist was better than the others. Wang decided to try a primitive form of echolocation; he took a bullet and a shuriken from his weapons belt and tossed the bullet off to the right. When it hit, a stream of machine gun fire sprayed the area where it landed, but Wang didn't care about that. Now he knew where the gun was.

Before the terrorist could react, Wang stood up and flung the shuriken toward the source of the sound, adjusting it minutely at the last moment so it flew directly into the terrorist's left eye socket. The terrorist got off one more wild shot, the bullets smashing a car's windshield in the parking lot, then he fell to the roof, dead.

Wang went out and retrieved the body, then dragged the corpse and the still living one back to where he had left the first one and the bomb. The first one had tried to get to his gun and fire it with his teeth; a noble gesture, but ultimately futile.

That gave Wang an idea, though. He took the two men who were still alive and used their turbans to tie their arms and legs together around the body of the third one. He tied their necks together so their heads were held snugly in front of the corpse's chest, then he used duct tape from the terrorists' bag to stick the bomb to the dead man's back. He twisted the timer's dial all the way around clockwise for its maximum delay: three hours. That should give him plenty of time to get airborne before the bomb went off.

He carefully snapped each of the bones in the live terrorists' fingers, then he grasped them by the neck and squeezed carefully until he crushed their larynxes. "Now," he said, "you may wonder how to keep bomb from blowing up." He removed their gags; without functioning vocal cords they didn't need those anymore, and for what he had in mind they would need their teeth. He said, "Lo Wang just give you fighting chance. If you can reach timer, you can keep turning it up until someone discovers you here."

He could see them think it through and arrive at the same conclusion. The only remaining appendages they possessed that they could grip anything with were their mouths, and the bomb was on the other side of a dead body.

Wang checked to make sure they couldn't loosen their bonds or wriggle around and reach the bomb from the side. He turned the terrorist bundle over so the live ones were on the bottom and the bomb was on top; that way if they didn't make it, the explosion would be softened by the three bodies and wouldn't do much damage to the building. Satisfied with his handiwork, he said, "It may be while before anyone comes help you, what with state of world these days, but don't worry, you not starve to death. It not pork, but Wang told it tastes like it."

The terrorists started tugging frantically at their bonds and gurgling through their crushed larynxes, but Wang merely shook his head and said, "If you not like it, think of people who must eat airplane food because I save their lives. Maybe that puts things in perspective."

He turned away and walked back over to his own bag of tricks, put most of his weapons back in the bag, then carried it up the other concourse until he came opposite the Quantas plane. He listened at air vents until he heard the sound of flushing, then climbed in and shinnied down, kicked the grate out the bottom, and dropped into a bathroom.

It was a women's room. Wang waited in the stall he had landed in until he was sure the coast was clear, then sauntered out into the concourse, but he startled a French woman who was just entering the bathroom. She stopped when she saw him, then automatically turned and entered the other door beside the one Wang had come out through. A moment later he heard her exclaim, "Aaa!" and a man said, "Hey!" but he didn't stick around to see how that turned out.

Chapter 11

"What kept you?" Flo demanded when he sat down next to her in the waiting area. She held two tickets in her hand. All the chairs but the one next to her were full; this was going to be a packed flight.

"I met freelance troublemakers on roof," Wang said. "Had to adjust their karma for them."

"Oh. Well, I got us tickets, but I had to buy first-class seats to do it. That's all they had left."

"That's good," Wang said. "Puts us closer to pilots."

She looked at him suspiciously. "What difference does that make? You're not going to hijack the plane, are you?"

"Ancient Japanese saying," Wang replied. "International flights seldom land in Australian outback."

She shook her head. "The ancient Japanese didn't know about airplanes *or* Australia."

Wang laughed. "How you know? Old ones very smart. Knew many things."

"Yeah, right. If you'd trusted Adams, he would probably have set you down right next to Ayers Rock."

"Wang trusted him once already. That was enough."

She shrugged and looked away. Wang looked around at the other passengers. Nervous, every one of them. Businessmen, vacationers, college kids; everyone wanted to be at home when the world went kablooey. Wang considered telling them that their salvation was on the same plane with them, but he didn't suppose anyone would believe him. And if they did, it would only blow his cover.

He could feel the ground shaking gently. It was worse now than it had been that morning. North and South America were growing closer by the minute. Fortunately Africa was staying put, shielding Spain somewhat from the seismic waves. When the big crunch came, however, this wouldn't be a good place to be. The middle of a continent would be the best place, and even that wouldn't be guaranteed safe.

It depended on the continent, of course. Wang suddenly realized why Dr. Exo had put his control center in central Australia. It was the loner among continents, far more isolated than the others. It would still be a quarter of the way around the world when the other continents fused together; Exo could ride out the shock waves in relative safety and then slide Australia gently into place after all the shaking was over.

It made perfect sense. Much more sense than Spain, which would be crushed like a bug on a windshield when Africa nudged northward under South America's impact. Too bad he hadn't thought of that before he had wasted his time here.

He looked over at Flo, sitting there beside him and fingering her tickets just as nervously as everyone else. She was still beautiful even so. Wang remembered the way her body had felt in the shower, the way she had clung to him in passion. Okay, so it hadn't been a total waste.

The flight crew was as eager to leave Spain as the passengers were; they got the plane loaded and on the runway in record time. Flo had bought a window seat on the right and the aisle seat next to it; Wang took the window seat and looked out as the gigantic airplane lumbered down the runway and hauled itself into the air. He craned to see the roof of the terminal building as they flashed past. There was something white up there, but he couldn't see at this distance whether the two men he had left tied up had started in on their unpleasant task. He would probably never know.

First class was definitely more comfortable than coach. Wang played with the tray and the telephone in the back of the seat in front of him, then leaned back in his seat and tried to take a nap. He needed all the rest he could get; he still hadn't recovered his full strength. But the moment he relaxed, the captain came on the intercom and said, "G'day, mates. This is Captain Willoughby saying thank you for flying with us today. We're presently climbing through twenty-five thousand feet toward our cruising altitude of thirty-seven thousand. Flight time today will be a little less than usual due to favorable winds and the shorter distance now that Australia is drawing close to the equator. We'll still have time for dinner, though, so sit back, relax, and enjoy the flight."

Wang looked at the other passengers. He could see the whites of their eyes all the way around their pupils as reality struck home: the world was being reshaped beneath them, and they were helpless to do anything about it. They were all within an inch of screaming and ripping off their clothes and attacking each other like caged rats, but they sat in their chairs and pretended to read the in-flight magazines and when the stewardesses came by and distributed their cellophane-wrapped meals they dutifully ate the food they could not taste.

How tenaciously people clung to the vestiges of civilization. Wang thought briefly of shouting "Fire!" just to see what would happen, but he decided against it. He wanted to make it to Australia before the continent crashed into India.

Once the flight was under way, Flo asked the stewardess for a pan of water so she could soak her feet. They were in first class; the stewardess didn't betray a bit of surprise. She just went into the galley and returned a moment later with a little plastic tray that might have been made for the purpose, and a bottle of mineral water.

"Thank you," Flo said.

Wang watched her set the tray on the floor and pour the water into it, then kick off her shoes and set her feet in the water. She leaned back in her chair, closed her eyes, and sighed.

"You are strange woman," he told her.

"You're resting your feet on a duffel bag full of weapons," she reminded him without opening her eyes. "Who's stranger?"

His bag of guns did make an uncomfortable lump at his feet. Even in first class there wasn't enough leg room these days. Wang slipped off his tabi, the split-toed sandals he always wore, and propped his feet up on top of his arsenal. He leaned back to nap, and this time he managed to drop into a fitful sleep.

He came out of it when the plane suddenly banked hard to the right. A harsh buzzing noise came from the cockpit. Wang thought at first that it was the sound of some vital piece of control machinery malfunctioning, but through the closed door he heard someone shout, "Collision alarm!" and someone else said, "Where, where? I don't see another plane anywhere!"

Wang looked out the window just as a streak of silver shot upward past it, only a foot or two ahead of the wing. He looked down at the column of smoke that receded rapidly behind them. It had been a surface-to-air missile!

That implied a surface somewhere below to shoot it from. Wang squinted through the hazy cloud cover and saw the faint outline of a beach, with waves breaking against it. They had reached Australia already.

The telephone in the seat in front of him gave out a shrill electronic warble. Wang ignored it, unzipping his duffel bag and pulling out the rocket launcher. He rummaged through the boxes of ammunition for heat-seeking missiles, snatched up half a dozen of them, and stood up.

Flo held the phone out to him. "It's for you," she said.

"This no time for—"

"It's Dr. Exo."

"—jokes. Oh." Wang took the phone from her outstretched hand and held it to his ear, half expecting it to blow up or shoot a needle into his brain. But no, if Exo had been able to booby-trap the plane before it left Spain, he wouldn't have been shooting missiles at it now.

"Hello?" he said.

"You Wang?" asked a shrill voice.

"No, you called me," Wang said.

"What?"

"You called me. Lo Wang."

"Soon to be Blown-up Wang!" the voice cackled. "This is your nemesis, Dr. Exo. I traced your pretty girlfriend's credit card and found your flight number, even your seat assignment. I have you in the palm of my hand. Prepare to die!"

"Shadow Warriors prepare for death since birth," Wang told him, keeping a wary eye out the window. "I doubt if you be one to make happen. First shot missed completely."

"That was a warning!" Exo said. "The next one will finish you."

Wang held the phone against his ear with his shoulder while he loaded the rocket launcher. "How much you like bet?"

"What?"

"Second time you say that. We must have bad connection. I ask, how much do you like bet? You know, put money where mouth is, as Americans say? You shoot down plane, you kill Wang, but if you don't, you pay. How about million dollars just to make good bet?"

"Are you crazy?"

"You right, million ridiculously low for man's life. Billion, then."

People in the seats around him were eyeing the rocket launcher and edging away, despite Flo's insistence that everything would be okay. "He's a professional," she told them. "Bad guys don't stand a chance against him."

One white-haired old lady smiled and said, "That's nice. When he's done here, do you think he could come on to Melbourne with me and help take care of a neighbor problem I've got there?"

"He's a little busy these days," Flo told her. "But I'll see what he can do."

Exo couldn't hear any of that through the telephone. He said, "A million, a billion, what does it matter; you'll never live to collect."

"You have big surprise," Wang told him. He spotted a bright spark moving swiftly up through the clouds. "Heh heh, got to go. See you on ground, Exo. Make sure you have money." He clipped the phone back into its rest in the seat, then turned to the passengers around him. "Now would be very good time to fasten seatbelts," he told them.

"What are you going to do?" Flo asked him.

"Shoot down Exo's ego," Wang replied. He turned toward the window and swung the butt of the rocket launcher at it. The plastic inner window shattered. The center window with the tiny hole at the bottom took two blows, but Wang knocked it out and cleared the rough edges away with the gun's shoulder brace. "Breathe out when glass breaks," he warned everyone, then he smashed the outer window.

Air shrieked out of the airplane. Sensors in the cockpit sounded the alarm, and bright yellow oxygen masks dropped down out of the overhead panels. The pilots immediately slowed the plane and began descending, which was good. Wang didn't want to stick his arms outside at five hundred miles per hour.

The rushing air tried to suck him outside. Wang let it take the rocket launcher and his forearms, letting his chest wedge against the hole. That put his head next to the window in front of the one he had knocked out; from there he could see outside fairly well.

The missile he had seen was coming in from the side. Wang felt the wind rushing against his arms, estimated the speed of the rocket and the speed of the plane, then fired. The heat-seeking antimissle lanced out and downward, curving in a gentle arc toward the rising warhead. The two met in a fiery blossom of destruction nearly a quarter mile away.

That was just the beginning. Missile after missile rose from the ground, reaching up to meet the descending airplane. They were coming from more than one site; Wang shot down the ones he could see on his side of the plane, then rushed over to the other side and busted out a window to shoot down the ones coming from there.

People were screaming inside the plane and struggling with their oxygen masks. Wang paid no attention to them, except for the burly man in the seat next to the window he had knocked out. He wore a plaid flannel shirt and had the perpetually stained and calloused hands of a backyard mechanic. Certainly a redneck, anyway. When the wave of missiles had all been knocked down, Wang pulled his arms back inside and asked him, "Can you shoot rocket launcher?" He had to shout to be heard over the rushing air.

"Why shore I can," the man said, grinning with tobacco-stained teeth. "Hate to meet somebody who couldn't."

"Here you go," said Wang, handing over the launcher. He dug out more ammunition from his bag and passed that over as well. "You keep that side clear, I take this one. Flo, you tell pilots to swing back and forth. That way Exo can't sneak shot at us from front or behind."

"Right," she said, unbuckling and staggering forward against the rushing wind.

Wang didn't have two missile launchers. The next best thing was the rail gun, which, fortunately, he had already reloaded. It didn't have heat-seeking projectiles, but that couldn't be helped. At least it was fast. He wouldn't have to lead the missiles as much as he would with a regular gun. He stuck his arms out the window again, pressed his face up against the next one, and waited for more missiles. The plane started banking hard from side to side; good, that meant the pilots were cooperating.

The second wave of missiles was not long in coming. Wang took careful aim, allowing for windage and elevation as best he could. His first couple of shots went wild, but he soon zeroed in on his targets, and

104

again the sky was filled with bright red puffs of fire. The redneck wasn't doing half bad, either. Of course with a heat-seeker it was pretty hard to miss, but you never could tell about a person until you saw them in action. Some people just froze up and wouldn't even pull the trigger.

The closer to the ground the 747 got the less time they had to shoot down incoming missiles, but there were fewer of them in the sky at any given moment so it evened out. Also, the plane was flying deeper and deeper into the interior of Australia; surely Exo didn't have air defenses all the way to Ayers Rock.

Wang turned his head forward for a moment and shouted toward Flo, "Tell pilots to fly right down next to ground! And aim for Ayers Rock."

"Okay!" She disappeared into the cockpit, then came back out a few seconds later. "They say they don't have authorization for that. Or a runway. They have to go to Sydney."

Wang saw a flicker of motion outside the plane. He had let a missile get too close while he was talking with Flo. He stuck his face back against the window and fired, but the plane zigged at just the wrong moment and he missed. And now the missile was directly behind the plane, where he couldn't reach it.

"Turn right!" he shouted. "Turn right!"

Flo echoed his order to the pilots, but it was too late. By the time the huge airplane had turned enough that Wang could see the missile again, it was nearly upon them. He fired the rail gun and this time he hit it, but the explosion was only a dozen feet behind the plane's tail. The 747's forward speed wasn't enough to leave the blast behind; a huge sheet of aluminum ripped off the rudder, and a piece of shrapnel punched through the elevator as well. Red hydraulic fluid began spewing out of the hole.

The plane lurched under the suddenly increased drag. Passengers screamed. Wang could feel in the pit of his stomach that they were going down.

Chapter 12

"Plane is hit!" he shouted. "Never make it to Sydney. It's Ayers Rock or nothing." Assuming they even made it that far. He scanned the sky for more missiles, saw one just at the edge of his field of vision heading for the other side of the plane.

"Incoming on your side," he called out to the redneck.

When he heard no response, he looked over at the seat where the man had been. Nothing remained but a scrap of red flannel caught against a jagged edge of glass and flapping in the wind. He had been sucked out.

Wang rushed over to that side of the plane and fired at the incoming missile. It took three shots, but he got it before it came close enough to do any more harm to the plane. He scanned for more, but that seemed to be it. When he was satisfied, he pulled back inside. To the woman sitting in the seat next to the empty one he said, "Very sorry. He was good shot."

"I suppose," she said, lifting her oxygen mask. "He was also a logger. A clearcutter. And he's been making crude passes at me ever since we took off. Good riddance, I say."

A clearcutter? Wang shuddered. Amazing what combination of skills and horrors lurked inside the same body.

"Keep eye out for more missiles," Wang told her. "But carefully. Shout for me moment you see any."

"Right." She leaned toward the window, but wisely left her seatbelt fastened tight.

"You too," Wang told the other first class passengers. "Watch for missiles. Your lives, and fate of world itself, depend on it."

Every oxygen-masked face pressed toward the windows. Good. Wang left them to the task and rushed into the cockpit, where the pilots were struggling to keep the plane flying straight and level.

"How bad is damage?" he asked them, stepping in past the navigator to look over the backs of the pilot's and copilot's seats at the banks of controls. The navigator shied away from him; maybe it was the bulky rail gun.

"We're losing hydraulic pressure to the elevators and rudder," the pilot said. "We can't fly without it."

"How far to Ayers Rock?"

"Ayers Rock, Ayers Rock," the copilot said. "What's so bleedin' important about Ayers Rock?"

"Nothing important," Wang told him. "Just control center for person who makes continents move."

"Oh. Well, we're about twenty minutes from it."

"Good. Take us down low as you can fly so we not make such good target. And land us as close to rock as you can. I will have to fight way in, so I like to start close."

"I?" asked Flo, who was standing beside the navigator. "I'm coming too, you know."

"I think it better you don't," Wang said. "No offense, but Wang move faster alone. You would be more use—"

She scowled. "No offense, but you're a chauvinist pig. I thought we were a team."

"We are. Sometimes team has better chance of getting what they want when they split up. I go in and draw attention of Exo's defenses, then after ten minutes you come after me and go straight for Exo himself. Stick your cute little .38 right up nose and pull trigger, if Wang hasn't already removed nose along with rest of his head."

She shuddered at the image. "So I'm supposed to be backup."

"Insurance," Wang said. "Hard to believe, but Wang not invincible. You my insurance that Exo still be stopped if something happens to me."

She gave him a look he couldn't decipher. It wasn't anger, nor concern, nor even disgust. It looked more like pity. He would have loved to ask her what that was all about, but just then the pilot said, "Bugger the hydraulics! They're finished."

"Everything, or just tail section?" Wang asked.

"Just the tail. The wing is still responding, for all the good it will do us."

"You can control attitude with flaps," Wang said.

The copilot scowled. "'You can control attitude

with flaps,'" he said mockingly. "You have any idea how hard that is?"

"Apparently too hard for you," Wang said, grabbing him by the collar of his shirt and dragging him from his seat. He shoved him out the cockpit door and propelled him over to the window he had busted out, turned him around, and stuck his back to the hole. The roar of air rushing out of the plane diminished by half. The copilot struggled to break free, but suction held him fast to the side of the plane.

"I control your attitude even without flaps," Wang said. He went back into the cockpit and sat in the copilot's chair. The pilot looked like he was going to protest, but Wang said, "There's another window just crying for plug," and the pilot closed his mouth.

Okay, then. Wang examined the controls. How hard could it be to fly a plane, anyway? It was all Bernoulli's principle acting on control surfaces; air rushing over curved wings producing lift. The U-shaped steering wheel angled the little flap thingies on the ends of the wings, tilting the plane sideways; pulling back on the same wheel did—did nothing, now that the hydraulics were gone. The foot pedals did nothing either. How about the throttles? There were four separate T-handles, all ganged together so they would move as one, but they could be unlocked and moved separately if you wanted. Wang tried one, and the plane slewed roughly to the right as he lowered the thrust on that side.

The pilot watched all this with a look of alarm. "You don't know how to fly, do you?"

"I do now," Wang said. He looked out the window. Tiny little things; why didn't they give pilots a better view, anyway? No matter, he could see well enough to land, if he could just find the landing site.

"All right," he said. "We coming up on it pretty soon, right?"

"Uhh . . . right," the pilot said. He turned to the navigator. "How long now, Bruce?"

Bruce pointed to their left, where a faint blue patch shimmered on the horizon. "There's Lake Mackay, so it can't be far. But there's a problem."

"Besides there being no runway, you mean?"

"Right. You see, Bruce, Australia is—"

"Wait a minute," said Wang. "I thought you Bruce."

"I am," said the navigator.

"But you just called pilot Bruce."

"Right. He's Bruce too. And so's the copilot."

"You joke, neh? What are odds of three Bruces?"

The pilot and navigator looked at one another, then burst out laughing. Bruce the pilot said, "This is your first time to 'Stralia, ain't it mate?"

"This matters how?" Wang asked, getting that perplexed sinking feeling in his stomach that he got when he knew he wasn't going to understand something.

"Not really, Bruce," said Bruce the navigator. He and Bruce the pilot burst into a fit of laughter.

They must be cracking under the pressure, Wang thought. He would probably have to fly the plane all the way down himself.

"Never mind," he said. He looked at Bruce the navigator. "You said we had problem. What is it?"

"The problem is, Australia is moving at about a hundred and fifty miles an hour northwest. We're going southeast. Even at our slowest landing speed, we can't come in from this direction. We'd break in half on the first bounce."

"Right," Bruce the pilot said. "Well, that's it then. Sorry. On to Sydney. We'll just have to try a water landing there." He pushed the throttle back into place.

Wang grabbed his hand and lifted it off the throttle. "I just showed you we can turn plane. If we circle around and come in from the southeast, ground speed will match our airspeed, yes? We could land gently as helicopter."

"Theoretically," said Bruce the pilot.

"You've got to be kidding," said Bruce the navigator. "You're talking about doing a carrier landing on a continent."

"Is that what you call it?" asked Wang. "I'm glad you have name for it, so musicians can write proper ballads to our heroism in years to come."

"What musicians? Nobody's going to know about us. We'll all be dead. Everybody else is going to be dead by the end of the day. Let us go home and be with our families one last time before it happens."

"I have better idea," said Wang. "Let's land this wounded albatross and save world instead."

Chapter 13

There was no missing Ayers Rock once it rose up above the horizon. Over a thousand feet high, a mile and a half long, and a mile wide, it stuck out of the plain like the fin on the back of a shark. It had a reddish tint to it, as if already stained by the blood that would soon flow in the caverns beneath it.

"All right, bring us around," said Wang. "Keep us low." He had decided to let the pilot do the flying as long as he obeyed orders.

They were only a few hundred feet up. Air still roared past the broken window just behind the cockpit. The ground seemed to race past below them, far faster than their airspeed alone would account for. It was just a blur of sagebrush and rocky ground, but as the plane turned gently to the left under the force of the uneven thrust from the engines, the difference between ground speed and airspeed gradually began to diminish.

"Good, good," Wang said, craning his neck to look out the window. Now the ground was moving little faster than it would beneath a car on a country road. But as he watched, the line of approach began to shift sideways and pick up speed again. "No, you turn too far," he said.

"I haven't done a bloody thing," the pilot told him. "We're headin' right for the bugger, straight along the direction of ground motion."

"The ground moves faster again," Wang said. "If plane is still on course, that must mean ground isn't."

"What are you talking about?"

"He means, Bruce," said the navigator, "that Australia has shifted course. It's heading straight north now." He looked at his instruments again. "Northeast, actually."

"It's Exo," Wang said. "He trying to keep us from landing by moving ground around underneath us."

"The entire *continent?*" asked the pilot. "That's impossible. The amount of energy that would take is so great it would melt the entire Earth."

"The Earth is already melted," said Flo. "Mostly, anyway. My mother's ABCD device merely borrows some of that energy and redirects it in a more efficient manner." She sounded smugly proud of her mother's accomplishment.

"Careening around the Indian Ocean is more efficient than what it was doing?"

"It depends on your point of view, I'm sure," she said. "I was just telling you how it's possible, that's all."

"Hah," snorted the pilot. "Well this Exo character can't turn a continent as fast as we can turn a plane, no matter how efficient his motor is. Bruce, call out the heading." He gripped the throttles and turned the plane toward the northeast.

They had already passed Ayers Rock. Wang considered ordering the pilot to take them around for another approach so they could land closer to it, but that would just give Exo more time to prepare another surprise for them. Better to land while they could and advance on the ground.

Exo swerved the continent around again, but the navigator kept them in line with its motion. Sagebrush drifted lazily past at only thirty or forty miles an hour. The 747 floated downward like a dandelion seed on a breeze. A hundred feet up, seventy-five, fifty . . .

"Landing gear down," said the pilot. The plane lurched slightly as he pushed the switch and the big wheels slid out of their compartments in the belly of the plane. The pilot picked up the intercom microphone and said, "G'day ladies and gentlemen, this is your captain speaking. At this time I would like to ask you to prepare for landing. It may be a bit bumpy due to the lack of a runway, but we'll do our best to keep the jouncing to a minimum. I will remind you, however, to use caution when opening the overhead compartments once we have come to a stop, as the contents may have shifted during—"

"We're going in," the navigator said.

"—landing. G'day, and thank you for flying Quantas." The pilot clipped the microphone back into place and grasped the control yoke, then almost casually brought the plane down until the wheels touched the ground.

The nose bounced upward violently, and the right wing dropped alarmingly close to the ground. Wang grabbed the wheel and straightened it out, but the pilot had already begun that motion and the combination of the two hands on the wheel made them overcorrect. The left wing arced downward into the ground, busting the outer twenty feet off like a brittle twig and slewing the plane around to that side.

"We're going to roll!" the navigator cried out. Wang looked back to see if Flo was safe, and saw that she had braced herself in the doorway. With her feet and hands wedged outward into the corners of the opening she looked a little like a tree seen through a window.

He turned back to the controls. The only things they had left that worked were the right aileron and the engines. That was enough; the captain snapped a switch labeled "thrust reverse" and the plane bounced to a stop in less than fifty feet. The right wing gouged a deep furrow in the ground and the plane listed a few degrees to that side, but other than that they were fine.

"Good landing," Wang said.

"Hah," said the pilot. "Quantas'll have my butt in a sling for this."

"You helping save world. I put in good word for you," Wang told him. He patted the pilot on the back and went into the first-class cabin.

Wind continued to whistle past the windows. It wasn't as strong as it had been during flight—Bruce the copilot had pried himself loose from the one he had been plugging—but there was still one heck of a headwind out there, enough to buffet the plane like

116

heavy turbulence. It was the wind from Australia's motion toward Asia.

"No time to lose," Wang said. "Come, Flo, must take care of Exo while there is still chance."

She gave him the look only a pained sidekick can give someone, but she shrugged and accompanied him back to his bag of weapons.

The passengers had clogged the aisles in their panic to escape the plane. There were no emergency exits on the upper deck, so people were shoving frantically toward the stairs.

"Hey!" Wang shouted over the hubbub, taking on a New York accent to cut through the noise. "Hey, hey, hey! Where you think you going? Only sagebrush and rock out there—and thousands of mutant beast men that Exo probably feeds poorly. You much better off staying here until this all over. And in the meantime, clear stairs!" He drew his sword and held it out in front of him, and people melted away between the seats again.

"That better."

The stewardesses had opened all the doors and emergency exits on the main level of the plane. That was probably a mistake; wind roared through the fuselage, blowing newspapers and magazines and old ladies' hats everywhere. Wang and Flo pushed their way up to the edge of the right-hand door. The bright yellow emergency slide was already out and inflated, but it was flapping in the wind like a flag. There was no way anyone could slide down that. A stewardess stood by the door to prevent anyone from trying it.

Wang estimated the distance to the ground. Thirty feet, anyway. He could probably jump and survive it,

Ryan Hughes

absorbing the shock in his legs and rolling when he hit, but Flo didn't have that kind of training.

With one quick slice of his sword he cut the emergency slide free. It whipped away in the wind and wrapped itself around the leading edge of the wing.

"You have rope ladders?" he asked the stewardess.

She nodded, her eyes wide in shock at the sight of an armed man on her airplane.

"Get me one," Wang said, but she didn't move. "Very sorry. *Please* get me one," he said, and he sheathed his sword.

The unexpected civility galvanized her into action; she dug into an emergency cabinet right beside the door and pulled out a coiled-up bundle of knotted rope and plastic foot treads with two metal carabiners sticking out of the coil. "These clip onto the pins that held the slide in place," she said, her voice barely audible over the wind.

"Good," Wang said, unclipping the last few inches of slide and hooking the rope in its place. He tossed it out and it unrolled into a ladder—also flapping straight backward. That didn't matter; Wang turned around and put his foot on the first rung, and the first section of ladder straightened out under his weight.

Wait a minute, he thought. There was an even better way, and it solved another problem as well: how to get his guns down. He tied the bag of weapons to the bottom of the ladder and lowered it to the ground. The rope still bellied out in the wind, but it was much easier to find the rungs now. Wang worked his way down, and Flo followed along while his weight held the ladder vertical. The wind whipped him around and bounced him against the airplane's alumi-

118

num skin, and when he reached the point where the belly began to curve underneath he was completely at the mercy of the gusts, but he fought to keep his footing and worked his way down to the ground.

One of the passengers tried to climb down behind Flo, but Wang waved him back and untied the duffel bag, letting the ladder swing rearward in the wind again. The passengers would be much safer in the plane.

The buffeting they had felt inside wasn't just wind. No matter how efficient the ABCD device was, you couldn't move a continent without scraping bottom occasionally. Or maybe that was Indonesia they were feeling, island after island plastering up against the northeast coastline.

"No time to lose," Wang shouted to Flo. "Let's go." He turned toward the tail of the plane.

With the wind at their backs, her hair whipped around her face until she caught it up in her hands and tied it in a knot. The sumo tuft on Wang's otherwise shaved head also caught the wind, but not enough to worry about. He and Flo walked down the length of the airplane until they stood beneath its tail and looked back at Ayers Rock.

It was a long way away. The extra minutes of flight they had spent maneuvering had taken them a dozen miles or so from it; only the top stuck up above the horizon. That meant a long walk, but fortunately the wind was at their backs. The distance was a plus in one respect, too. If they didn't go directly for the Rock, Exo wouldn't know what angle they were coming from, so he would have to spread out his army to intercept them.

The vegetation was rough and sparse enough that quite a bit of bare ground showed through. Rocks lay scattered at random among the bushes and grass, making the footing just uneven enough that a person had to keep their eyes on the ground to avoid tripping.

Wang unloaded most of the weapons from his bag and strapped them on to make carrying them easier. Dual Uzis in holsters over the shoulders, riot gun in a sheath along his left leg, grenade launcher on the right, rail gun across his chest, and shuriken, grenades, sticky bombs, caltrops, and all the other hand-held gadgets he could fit all along the loops on his belt. Night vision goggles, binoculars, and medkit went into pockets. He tucked ammunition in every spare crevice, but he continued to carry the much-lightened bag.

"You mean there's more in there?" Flo asked incredulously. "What could possibly be left?"

"Oh, just more of same," Wang said casually. He didn't want to worry her needlessly. He was nearly sure he wouldn't need the pocket nuclear bomb, but you never knew.

Chapter 14

They should have brought water. The hot wind blowing across the outback sucked the moisture right out of them. A candy bar or two would have been nice, too. Even a few bags of airline peanuts. It was too late to go back for any now, but Wang berated himself for foolishly leaving without stocking up. He had allowed himself to rush, and this was the result. He wondered what other vital supplies he had forgotten.

The 747 was a small glint of silver in the distance behind them. Ayers Rock was a big bump in the distance in front of them. They were marching a bit to the left of it, staying behind a line of low bushes whenever they could in the hope that they might come around from the north end without alerting anyone. It was probably a futile attempt; anybody on top of the Rock with a pair of binoculars could see them coming for miles, but it was the only thing Wang could think of that might possibly give them an advantage.

"Must you walk so fast?" Flo asked after the first couple of miles.

"Ancient Japanese saying," Wang told her. "He who hesitates is last."

"Ancient Japanese saying, my ass," she said. "Slow down."

"As you wish." Wang slowed his pace, but not by much. He wanted to get there and finish the job, not wander through the outback with his tongue hanging out for another hour or two.

That was not to be. Less than a mile later, he heard a rattle of rock and a sharp exclamation from behind him, and turned to see Flo on the ground cradling her left foot in her hands.

"What's the matter? What happened?" he asked, bending down to help her up.

She didn't try to stand. "I twisted my ankle. The wind caught me while I was stepping over a rock and blew my foot away from where I was trying to step." She moved it carefully from side to side. "Ow!"

Wang bent down in front of her and ran his hands over her leg and foot. Her skin felt warm and smooth beneath his own, but he ignored the sensations that passed through him at her touch and concentrated on feeling for damage. He couldn't feel any broken bones, but when he pressed against the tendons she cried out in pain. He pressed again, trying to isolate which one it was, but she cried out again when he pushed on a different one.

"Which one is it?" he asked. "This, or—"

"Ow! That one!"

He had pushed on a third.

122

"You could not pull three different tendons," he said. "Let's try again. This one, or—"

"Let's not," she said. "It hurts; let's leave it at that, okay?"

"If I can find which one it is, I can use acupressure to ease pain," he told her.

"Look, it's a pulled muscle. It's going to hurt. Just give me a minute to get my strength back, okay?"

Wang nodded, impressed. She was willing to go on despite her pain; that was the mark of a good warrior.

She didn't look good, though. On top of her injury, she was obviously dehydrated. Her face drooped, her shoulders slumped; even her hands looked dry and slack, like wilted leaves on a tree. It took more like five minutes before she was ready to go on, and even then she had a decided limp, but when he asked her if she thought she could make it all the way with that injury she said, "I don't really have much choice now, do I?" and kept hobbling along.

They had one other option: Wang could carry her. He gauged the distance and his own strength and came to the unfortunate conclusion that he wouldn't be much good for anything when he got there if he tried it. But at this rate Australia would smash up against Africa by the time they reached the Rock, much less found Exo's lair beneath it. Wang fidgeted, pulling one weapon after another from his arsenal and holding each one out in front of him experimentally. He itched to start something, to get into it with this megalomaniac Dr. Exo, but he couldn't leave his sidekick behind.

There was only one thing to do: If he couldn't take

the fight to Exo, then he had to bring the fight out here into the scrub brush. He would have picked someplace with more cover if he'd been able to choose his battleground, but this would have to do. At least it offered Wang the same advantage that it offered Exo: He would be able to see his enemies coming miles away.

He pulled out his grenade launcher. He wished the logger hadn't taken his rocket launcher with him when he'd been sucked out the window. That would have been the best weapon for what Wang had in mind. The grenade launcher would do, though. He armed a grenade and stuck it into the barrel.

"What are you doing?" Flo asked.

"Calling us a taxi," he replied.

He fired the grenade on a high arc toward Ayers Rock. It fell far short, but it made a nice explosion in the prairie. Wang fired a couple more, hoping it would look to the scouts on top of the Rock as if a battle were going on out there. There was one other effect he hadn't counted on: The dry brush caught fire from the explosions and the wind fanned it into a solid wall of flame racing toward the Rock.

Flo shuddered at the sight of the explosions and the fire. "Maybe you can explain to me how that's going to help us," she said.

"Watch," Wang told her, not sure if it would do anything at all other than send smoke into Exo's ventilation shafts, but he had hopes.

They kept walking. The wind kept blowing. The ground kept shaking. Occasionally they would feel an earthquake wave pass through, feeling for all the world like an ocean wave the way it tilted them first forward, then back as it passed beyond them.

Finally Wang saw a flicker of motion burst through the flames. Two, no, three ground vehicles of some sort racing toward them. He smiled. "There is how it helps us. Get ready to fight."

She pulled her .38 from its holster, but he handed her one of his Uzis instead. "Too many of them for that," he said.

She scowled at that news, but she took the Uzi. "Aren't we even going to hide and ambush them?" she asked.

"They might miss us," Wang said. "You can't run with bad ankle, so we have to make sure they come close." So saying, he plucked a grenade from his belt, pulled the pin, and tossed it a few dozen yards away to his right, where it exploded with a bright flash. More bushes caught fire there, and Flo shied away even more strongly than before.

"Don't worry," Wang said, wondering why she was so afraid of fire. She must have had a bad experience with it once. "The wind will blow it ahead of us," he said, pointing to the way the fire raced off in a slowly widening front toward the Rock. It didn't stop burning at the source; the flame front actually expanded into a line of fire that kept burning from the point where it had started all the way to the leading edge, but it was clear that it wasn't going to burn sideways toward them in this wind.

That gave Wang an idea; he estimated where the advancing vehicles would be when they met the flame front, then he lobbed another grenade to the left. It exploded and started another fire, which leaped from bush to bush in a line parallel to the first one, leaving a clear path of unburned prairie between them. A perfect highway for the vehicles—Wang could see now that they were tanks—to take if they wanted to reach Wang and Flo without driving through fire and smoke again.

Wang kept walking toward them. Flo walked nervously beside him, hardly limping at all now that her mind was so focused on the oncoming tanks.

"Shouldn't we take cover?" she asked.

"No need." Wang examined the tanks as they approached. They looked U.S.-made. Wang didn't know one type from another, but they were boxy and painted olive drab. Exo must have bought them surplus. The lower half was mostly treads with the body slung between them, and the upper half was an oblong gun turret with a four-inch cannon sticking out well beyond the body. A driver inside peered out through a slit so he could see where he was going, and the gunner had the same arrangement to see where he was shooting. Not accurate at all on the move; it would be tough to hit Ayers Rock with one if they were going in the other direction.

The first of them was maybe a quarter mile away when it opened fire. Dirt and rocks flew up in a fountain a few hundred feet ahead of Wang and Flo. The second tank fired and hit close to the same spot. The third, quite a way behind the others, overcompensated and blasted a bush a dozen yards behind them. Fires spread from those hits as well.

Flo ran to the left to avoid the wall of flame that now raced right for them from the last shot. Wang took his time following her, judging relative speeds and moving clear just as he felt the heat of the fire roaring past.

The tanks' first shots had ruined their approach corridor. Smoke and flame hid their quarry from them as they drew closer, but Wang could hear the whine of their engines and feel the vibration from their metal treads. Finally the leader burst through the flames. Burning brush flew outward and overhead, and dirt billowed out behind it as it churned up the ground.

The driver had been running blind in the smoke. He had drifted a bit to the left, and it took him a moment to get his bearings and swing around. Wang didn't give him the time; he fired a grenade into the treads and watched the tank swerve to the side when the explosion tore apart the running gear.

The turret still worked, but not for long. Wang holstered the grenade launcher and pulled out his Uzi, aiming for the end of the cannon. It had a far bigger bore than the beer bottles he had impressed his union friends with back in America; he fired a short burst of bullets straight down the barrel without even aiming carefully. He put a bullet in the barrel of the machine gun that stuck out above the cannon, just in case, then he holstered the gun again and thumbed his nose at the tank.

The cannon lowered until it was pointed straight at Wang's chest. The gunner fired.

Unfortunately for him, a dozen or more flattened slugs wedged against the shell kept it from moving down the barrel. The force of its propellant had to go somewhere; Wang heard a muffled thump from inside the tank and smoke belched out the viewports. He watched to see if anyone tried to open the hatch, but the explosion had evidently gotten them all.

"We now have taxi," he said to Flo. "Rest your poor, tired feet. Maybe even give them good soak if tank carry water."

"Oh, tank you," she said.

Wang looked at her askance. "Ancient Japanese saying: Pun is lowest form of humor."

She laughed. "Ancient Chinese saying: No pun, no fun."

"You make that up," he said.

"And you didn't?"

"Wang not say that."

He led the way up to the smoking wreck. It would provide good cover against the others. He dropped his bag of weapons at the base of it while he and Flo climbed up onto the body and peered around the turret, but they were blown back to the ground by a point-blank blast from the next tank. They knew where the obvious cover was, and they were making sure Wang and Flo couldn't use it.

Well, Wang could use that to his advantage as well. While they pummeled the dead tank, he could try something else. He picked himself up and dusted himself off, then pointed to the right. "Go around that way," he told Flo. "Shoot at slits they look through." He lobbed another grenade toward the attacking tank to create a diversion, then sprinted left through the smoke cloud from the explosion until he came alongside its clanking treads. He leaped up onto the fender, then crawled forward until he could see the driver's viewport.

An Uzi barrel fit neatly into the slit. Wang sprayed the interior of the tank, wincing as bullets ricocheted overhead from the turret, which Flo was spraying with her Uzi.

"Enough!" Wang yelled down to her. When she stopped shooting he stood up and fired into the gunner's turret point blank, then just for good measure he jumped up to the top, opened the hatch, and tossed a grenade inside. He felt the concussion, but the tank kept moving. It was headed straight for the other tank.

Wang climbed through the hatch and dropped down through the turret into the main compartment, but the gunner's and the driver's bodies got in his way and he couldn't reach the controls before the tank's forward motion drove the cannon directly into the side of the other one, bending it like a nail hit off center.

"Damn, we needed that!" Wang yelled. He pulled back on the throttles and the tank shuddered to a stop, then he climbed back out to help Flo inside. If nothing else, it would provide mobile cover.

The third tank was closing on them fast. A cannon shot blasted a hole in the dead tank in front of them, and shrapnel whizzed past as Flo scrambled up and into the turret. Wang jumped in after her and dogged the hatch, then went for the controls.

Flo had already pulled away the driver's body. Wang sat in the chair and pulled back on the control levers, and the tank backed away from the other one, trailing its broken cannon like a bent soda straw. He shoved one lever forward and kept the other back, and the tank whirled around to face the oncoming one.

Its cannon fired, and the tank they were in rang with the impact. It hadn't been a direct hit; the shot didn't penetrate, but Wang didn't want to give them another chance. He shoved both throttles forward and the tank lurched up to speed, curving around the other one faster than Exo's henchmen could keep up with their turret gun. They tried holding still and firing as Wang's tank swept past, but they missed.

The standoff couldn't last all day, though. Wang couldn't shoot at them from inside the damaged tank, and eventually they would get lucky if they just kept firing at him as he came around.

"Here, take controls," he said to Flo. "This is left track lever, and this is right. Just keep doing what we do now."

She looked dubious, but she said, "Okay," and slid into the seat.

Wang climbed up into the turrret, threw open the hatch, and stuck his head out, but a machine gun bullet through his sumo tuft persuaded him to be a bit more cautious. He stuck his riot gun over the lip and fired at the other tank, trusting to the law of averages that a few of the buckshot balls would make it through the view slits. They might not kill anybody, but they would make the gunner duck for cover. He braced his boots on the ladder while he reloaded—no sense attacking without a full clip—then he fired another shot and leaped out of the turret.

The other tank's cannon barrel was sweeping around toward him as the gunner tried to target him again. Wang fired another shot from the riot gun to keep whoever else was inside the other tank from shooting small caliber stuff at him, then when the turret gun came close enough he leaped, caught it, and wrapped his legs around it.

Just then the gunner fired it. Wang felt his hands go numb from the concussion, but he hung on and shinned his way up to the base of the barrel. Hanging upside down from it, he pulled his Uzi again and sprayed bullets in through the driver's viewport, then twisted around to shoot into the gunner's ports.

The gunner beat him to it. Wang saw a flash, and a bullet tore a furrow across his chest. Another one punched a hole through his left arm. His biceps spasmed with the shock and he slipped from the barrel, hit the side of the tank, and fell to the ground—right in front of the advancing treads.

Chapter 15

Wind whipped dirt and smoke every which way. The roar of tank engines and the clatter of treads against rocks was almost deafening. Wang saw a cleated metal track coming straight for him and he rolled to the side just in time to avoid being crushed, but that put him right in the path of the tank Flo was driving. The two tanks were grinding past each other only a foot or so apart. Wang made himself as small as possible and undulated between the idler wheels as they passed.

The one he had attacked was moving straight ahead now, driverless. Wincing with the pain in his left arm, Wang grabbed the back of it as it roared by and pulled himself up onto its steel deck again. He hugged the turret this time so nobody could get another shot at him without opening the hatch. There were hand-holds and a little railing at the back that made it easy to hang on.

The gunner inside knew Wang was on his tank. He

swiveled the turret this way and that, fired the machine gun, even fired the cannon again, but Wang held on tight. He reached up with the Uzi and sprayed bullets in through the viewports, but this gunner was smart enough to stay out of the way.

Eventually the tank ground to a halt. Unless there were three people in the tank, and there had been only two in the other one, that meant the gunner had gone down to the driving controls. Wang sprang to the top of the turret and tried the hatch, but it was dogged from inside.

Flo brought the other tank to a halt, too. The two iron beasts rumbled side by side like tired dinosaurs resting in mid battle, neither one able to damage the other enough to finish it.

Wang looked down at his chest and arm. Blood flowed freely from both wounds. He would need that; he took a moment to constrict the vessels leading to the affected tissue and the bleeding stopped. He flexed his left hand and was pleased to see that the fingers still worked. He wouldn't be able to count on that arm for much strength, though, not with a hole right through the biceps.

And he hadn't even gotten within a mile of Ayers Rock yet. This wasn't promising.

He shook his head. No negative thoughts. Bad attitude lost more battles than bad odds. He had to concentrate on the task at hand, one step at a time, and eventually he would find Dr. Exo in his gunsights.

First he had to finish off this damned gunner. Wang tried to think how to do it, but the guy was sealed in tight. Poison gas might reach him, but Wang had no poison gas, and the wind would probably blow it away before it could penetrate the gunports in any case.

There had to be a way. Think. Master Shoji would be laughing his head off about now, watching his student sit there like a squirrel with a can of nuts, trying to figure out how to get at the soft goodies inside.

So how do you open a can of nuts? Wang asked himself. With a can opener, of course. That implied that Wang needed a tank opener. But what did a tank opener look like?

He examined the outside of the tank for clues. The gunner inadvertently helped him out by swiveling the turret around, trying to lower the cannon enough to shoot at Flo's tank with it. She was too close; the barrel banged into the side of her turret.

Wang had to raise his legs to avoid the tool box as he swept by. It was bolted to the top of the track fender on the right side, a rectangular metal box painted the same drab green as the rest of the tank. It had a few holes in it from Wang's riot gun. Apparently the designers didn't figure tools were important enough to protect from battle damage; they had probably never had to pay for their own five-hundred-dollar hammer.

Hmm. Maybe he could unbolt the exhaust pipe and re-route it into the tank's interior. That would be a perfect way to gas the gunner . . . provided Wang had about two hours to wait for him to die. The world didn't have two hours. Wang had to snuff this guy *now* and get on with his mission.

What else, what else? He could fill the cannon full of wrenches and coax the gunner into shooting at him, but he wanted to capture this tank intact if he could. It would get them a lot farther past Exo's defenses if they could fight their way in with a four-inch cannon.

He leaned out and flipped open the toolbox. The top tray held an assortment of wrenches and screwdrivers; Wang grabbed a crescent wrench and a Phillips screwdriver before the turret swung him around out of reach again.

Wang looked for bolts or screws in the armor plate, but there were no obvious joints. What use was a crescent wrench or a screwdriver against two-inch armor? What use were they against anything? If he could get the hatch open he could brain the gunner with the wrench or stab him in the heart with the screwdriver, but other than that they were useless.

He was just about to toss them to the ground when the thought hit him: If he could get the hatch open. Idiot! The hatch was on hinges, and the hinges opened outward. He examined the hinges, and sure enough, he could reach the pins with the screwdriver. They were welded into the stationary side of the hinge, but that didn't matter. Wang set the end of the screwdriver against the center of the hinge pin and whacked it with the crescent wrench. It left a little dimple in the pin. Wang whacked it harder.

The gunner whirled the turret around when he heard the pounding. He fired his machine gun at the flat side of Flo's tank, apparently hoping the bullets would ricochet off and hit Wang, but the angle was wrong for that. Wang kept pounding, and finally the first hinge pin busted loose. He punched it all the way out, then started in on the other one, but the plastic handle of the screwdriver shattered under the blow.

135

He had to hold the screwdriver shaft in his fingers and pound on that, but he had just gotten started when the gunner began swinging the turret around again in an attempt to shake him off, and Wang had to use at least one hand to hang on to the railing at the back of the turret.

"Stop trying to swing Lo!" he shouted, banging on the tank's armored sides, but the gunner ignored him.

He needed another hand. Or—wait a minute. No he didn't. He had learned something from a desperate terrorist just this morning: nobody was without an appendage to grip with if they still had their head.

He clamped onto the railing with his teeth. The tank's vibration transmitted all the way through his skull. The sound waves in his eyeballs blurred his vision, but Wang found the hinge pin by feel and pounded on it for all he was worth. Finally it gave way. Wang dropped the tools and grabbed the railing with his hand again, snatched an Uzi from its holster, and forced open the hatch.

Machine gun fire ricocheted off the metal and bounced just past Wang's head. Good trick, but two could play that game. He angled the hatch so the outgoing ricochets would spray harmlessly to the side, then he held his Uzi nearly in the stream of bullets and fired at the same spot on the hatch.

He heard a scream from inside and wrenched the hatch all the way off. He nearly stood up to put a few final bullets into the gunner's wounded body, but he stopped before his head cleared the opening. That scream hadn't sounded sincere enough. Wang waved his hand over the opening, and sure enough, more bullets flew out.

"Tricky, tricky," Wang muttered, taking a sticky bomb from his belt and arming it. It was proximity fused, designed to attach to a doorway or a wall and blow up when someone passed by, but it would work fine in motion, too. Wang dropped it inside the tank, and it exploded before it hit bottom. This time the screams were genuine, if short lived.

Wang climbed in and heaved the two bodies out through the hatch, then beckoned to Flo to come on over. She crawled out of the other tank and he helped her into the good one, noting as she came down the ladder that her sprained ankle seemed much better now. A little rest had helped; that was good. She might need to use it hard again before the day was over.

He went over to the first tank and retrieved his bag of weapons and ammunition, tossed it down through the hatch, then followed it down. The interior of the tank was heavily damaged from the bomb blast, but the vital controls still worked. They could drive and they could shoot; Wang couldn't ask for much more. He seated himself in the driver's chair and turned the tank toward Ayers Rock, then ran the throttles up to full speed.

The fires had mostly burned themselves out by now, but smoke still rolled from the burned patches of prairie. Wang deliberately aimed for one of the long burned swaths and drove down the middle of it. The smoke might hide their approach and give them the advantage of surprise when they encountered whatever defenses Dr. Exo had set up closer to the Rock.

Even at full speed, the smoke blew out ahead of

them in the wind. Some of it came into the tank, but not enough to make them move out into the open again.

While Wang drove, Flo dug through the interior of the tank, looking for anything that might be useful. She found racks of ammunition for the cannon, belts of machine-gun cartridges, grenades, and all sorts of other weapons, but the most useful thing she discovered was in a miscellaneous storage bin: food and water.

The water was in an oblong canteen. She opened it and took a long gulp, then poured some over her head. She tilted back so it would splash onto her face, then she opened her mouth and poured some more straight down her throat without even swallowing.

Wang laughed, but when she showed no sign of stopping he said, "Hey, careful with that. You not only one thirsty, you know."

She tilted the canteen back upright. "Oh. Sorry. Here." She handed it over. It held about two swallows.

"Is there any more?" Wang asked when he had finished it.

She checked the storage bin. "Uh . . . no," she said. "Sorry. There's food, though." She held up an oblong package about an inch thick and four or five inches long.

"What is it?"

"Hard to say. It's labeled Field Ration number four two seven B." She turned it over. "Oh, here we go. Irradiated pasteurized processed cheese food product."

"Gack!" Wang said. "They call that food? Master

Shoji taught me never eat anything with Product in name."

"That's all there is," Flo said.

"Then Lo Wang fight on empty stomach."

Flo looked at the label again, then put the ration packet back in the storage bin. "Me, too."

Wang peered out into the smoke, trying to see anything but gray. He was about to give up when a dark man-shaped figure loomed up out of the swirling cloud and swept past only a few feet to the left. Wang heard a startled "Hey!" as the tank roared past. He tried to make sense of what he had seen. It had looked like a man in a cheap brown American business suit.

"I think we just about run over tourist," Wang said.

"Good riddance," Flo replied.

Indeed, thought Wang. Tourists were the least of their problems. They would face much worse when they got to Exo's lair.

"Do you know how to fire cannon?" he asked.

"How hard can it be?"

"Army recruits spend months in training for it."

"Only months? Piece of cake, then." She stood up inside the turret and Wang heard metal latches open and close, then the gun swung around left and right. When it pointed forward again a loud boom rocked the tank.

"You figure it out good," Wang said.

"Like I told you, piece of cake."

"Get ready to fire again. We draw close to Rock." Wang could see its dark outline looming up through the smoke. He veered left until he drove out of the smoke column and looked quickly for other vehicles. There they were, at least a dozen tanks lined up at the base of the rock waiting for them. Wang drove back into the smoke.

The other tanks opened fire, and the ground on either side of them erupted in fountains of dirt and rock and burning brush. Wang steered farther to the right, deeper into the smoke. He kept going until it started to clear again. "Get ready," he said to Flo.

They burst out into clear air again. Another dozen tanks were waiting on that side of the smoke, but one of them was already aflame. Wang wondered who had done that to it, then he realized what had happened and he laughed. "Lucky shot!" he called out.

Flo saw it, too. "Who says it was luck?" she asked playfully.

"You do it again, it not luck." Wang brought the tank to a stop to give her better aim.

The cannon roared. A moment later dirt blew up just in front of the tank next to the one she had hit with her test shot.

"Ancient Japanese saying," Wang said. "Beginner's luck only strike once."

She didn't reply. He heard the breech open and close, then another shot shook the tank. This time the one she had missed earlier rocked backward under a direct hit. Its turret slewed sideways and the gun dropped to the ground.

"Still think it was luck?"

"The first one." Wang started the treads again and ducked back into the smoke, and not a moment too soon. The tanks that hadn't been damaged all fired their cannons, and shells fell all around them as they raced for cover.

There was no way to fight that many tanks directly.

Wang kept driving down the smokey path of the fire while they blasted away at where they thought he might be, but he knew dumb luck could work in their favor just as easily as in Flo's. He had to get out of the line of their fire. Trouble was, there was no way to do that now that they knew where he was, so he did the next best thing.

He stopped the tank again.

"What are you doing?"

"Letting place where they *think* we are move ahead of where we really are."

The pounding of shells moved away. A few stragglers still landed nearby—and one hit close enough to rock the tank—but none hit directly. After a minute or so, Wang moved ahead again, driving slowly.

The smoke grew thicker the closer to the Rock they came. The fire had been wider here, and the air was more turbulent near the great mass of conglomerate rock; the smoke stuck around longer. That could work to Wang's advantage, if he could just figure out where he was.

"Turn gun sideways," he said, peering to see anything through the smoke. He suppressed a cough. It was getting pretty thick inside the tank now, too.

Flo turned the cannon to the right, and not a moment too soon. A wall of rock suddenly appeared out of the smoke. Wang hauled back on the throttles, but too late; the tank slammed into the rock, tilting upward for a second before it rolled backward and settled onto the ground again. "Damn!" he said, "I'm running into walls now!"

If they hadn't turned the gun away, they would have rammed it straight into the rock. But they had, and now Wang knew right where he was. He turned the tank sideways and drove slowly along the edge of the rock face. A dark spot loomed out of the smoke, and he nearly ordered Flo to fire at it, but then he realized it was a shallow cave. It was no surprise; the base of Ayers Rock was riddled with them.

This one was hardly a cave, really. Just a hollow in the rock. But Wang smiled when he saw it. It was big enough to shield a tank.

He stopped just short of it, with the tank still aimed along the edge of the Rock. "Shoot level to ground directly ahead," he said.

"Roger." Flo fired the cannon.

"I am not Roger. I am Lo Wang. Now turn around and shoot in other direction."

She laughed. "Whatever you say. Bruce." But she swiveled the cannon around and fired again.

Wang heard her second shot strike metal. One of the tanks lined up on that side had just taken a hit. Quickly, he shoved the throttles forward and steered the tank into the hollow.

A barrage of cannon fire came from the other tanks beside the one that Flo had hit. Wang heard explosions, then return fire from the tanks on that side. Both forces were firing blind into the smoke, aiming in the direction they saw shots coming from. Aiming right at each other.

Wang leaned back and stretched. "I love it when this happens." His wounded arm protested the stretching and he gave it up, but he kept his smile.

"Oh, yeah, like how often does this happen, anyway?" Flo asked sarcastically.

"This is first time, actually," Wang admitted. "But I am happy enough."

They could hear a pitched battle going on now. Cannon fire was almost constant, and the clang and boom of explosive shells sounded like popcorn in a metal popper. Like popcorn, it reached a crescendo, then began to diminish until there was only one bang every few seconds. The sole survivor was making sure he had hit his target.

Wang edged the tank out of the niche in the rock just enough for Flo to aim the cannon. "Focus on sound," he told her. "Close eyes and listen. Find his position. Now fire."

The cannon roared. The moment she fired, Wang pulled back into cover just in case, and it was a good thing he did. There was a bright flash that lit up the inside of the tank even through the tiny view slits, and a roar like the end of the world. The ground shook for ten seconds afterward.

"What did you hit?" Wang asked incredulously.

Flo pulled her head down from the turret. She was wearing a sheepish grin. "Uh, actually, I think it wasn't what I hit so much as what I shot. I grabbed a different kind of shell from another bin by mistake. It fit the gun, so I didn't think it would make that much difference."

"Let me guess. This one had three triangles inside circle stamped on side."

She checked in the ammo bin to see. "Yeah, that's right."

Wang nodded. "How many more of them we have?"

"Just one. They're nukes, aren't they?" She sounded awe-stricken that she had fired such a thing.

He pulled the tank out of its hiding place and drove away from the site of the explosion. "It was just little one," he said. "Nothing to worry about."

"Oh, I suppose you use them all the time."

"No," said Wang. "They're not personal enough."

She gave him one of *those* looks, so he decided to yank her chain a little. Choosing his words carefully, he said, "The sword is personal. When slicing through a man, you get that personal feedback. Nuclear weapons, neh—" he shrugged. "Goes off, big bang, and you don't get any feeling. Where's sport in that?"

She didn't answer. He drove out of the smoke past the mangled hulks of the tanks that had been hit by their own friendly fire. How many more waited beyond the next smoke cloud?

"There's no sport in them," he repeated, "but load the next one just in case."

Chapter 16

There were more caves than you could shake a *bo* at. As they drove around the perimeter of Ayers Rock, Wang began to wonder if it would be possible to find the right one. He was certain at least one of them led to Exo's underground command center, but there were no obvious roads, no elevator doors standing open, nothing to indicate which particular pock in the monolith might hold the doorway to Exo's lair.

There were no more tanks waiting for them, either. Now that they were clear of the smoke, the place looked like it might on any day after the tourists had gone. The time of day was right. The sun was in the northwest already; what with the plane flight eastward it had been a short day. There might be another hour or two of light left, but no more.

The rock changed color as the angle of light shifted. The weathered surface had been bright red when they arrived; now it was amber with gold highlights. Wang peered into each fissure and cave as they passed, but none bore evidence of habitation. He looked at the tank tracks that criss-crossed the plain, hoping to see where they originated from, but that was no use either. Exo had played so many war games out here—and so many tourists had driven around the Rock in their Land Rovers—that tracks led everywhere.

So this was Exo's second wave of defense: no defense at all. He didn't need one if Wang couldn't find the door.

They needed a guide. "I can't believe it," Wang muttered. "When I don't kill someone, they come back, haunt me. When I finish everyone off, turns out I should have kept one alive to ask directions. Not fair."

"Life's not fair, honey," said Flo. She was speaking from experience: She had bowed to her hunger and opened the bar of cheese food product, but she put it back after the first bite.

"I think it's time we make our own entrance," Wang said. "See that cave there?" He turned the tank so it was headed toward the rock again and pointed to the largest of three dark openings at its base.

Flo looked over his shoulder and squinted through the driver's view slit. "Yeah, I see it."

"I back up little ways, then you shoot it with nuke. Make big bang, open up path for us."

"If it doesn't destroy the whole damned fortress," she said.

"That fine, too," Wang said. "A Shadow Warrior accepts victory, whatever form it takes." He turned the tank around and drove away from the Rock a mile or so, then turned around again. "Think you can hit it from here?" he asked.

"I don't know. Maybe."

"Maybe not good enough when we only have one shot. Get range with one of other shells."

"Right." Flo stood back up in the turret, opened the cannon's breech, and exchanged shells. The barrel rose a bit, angled slightly left, then the cannon roared. A puff of smoke blew away in the wind; Wang peered past it and saw an explosion on the side of the rock to the right of the cave.

"Little more to left."

Flo tried it again, and this one fell short.

"Again."

The third shot lit up the inside of the cave. Fire belched out of it for a second, then subsided. "Very good. Now use nuke."

"Are you sure we're far enough away?"

"Of course I sure," Wang said. He certainly hoped they were. They would know in a minute.

"Okay then, here goes." Flo loaded the shell, closed the breech, and fired.

Wang ducked down so he wasn't in the path of the view slits. Brilliant white light filled the inside of the tank for a second, and he heard a roar transmitted through the ground. Then the air wave passed over them, a crackling wall of sound that shoved the tank back from air pressure alone. The ground began to shake.

Then the debris started raining down. The tank rang like the inside of a bell as chunks of rock smashed into it. Dents appeared in the armor as if an angry god were trying to kick his way in. Wang leaped out of the driver's chair just in time to avoid being crushed.

He recognized his mistake immediately. He had directed Flo to shoot for a cave so the mass of Ayers Rock overhead would direct the blast downward, but this cave was evidently not as deep as it looked. It must have been a rough parabola, which meant that an explosion at the mouth of it would be focused outward as well as downward by the curved walls. It hadn't been that big a nuke, but they were in the direct path of the blast.

"Get down!" he yelled to Flo, who had braced herself against the back of the turret. He grabbed her legs and pulled them out from under her just as another impact wrenched the turret free. Daylight streamed in through the ragged opening, as did a landslide of rocks and dirt.

The tank took another hit so hard that it skidded around and tipped on its side. Wang was afraid it would go on over and trap them inside, but the battering died down and it remained standing precariously on its left tread.

"Out. Now," Wang said, slapping Flo on the butt to get her moving. She crawled out through the hole where the turret used to be. Wang grabbed up his gun bag and followed her.

They stood beside the tank, their ears ringing and their bodies bruised. A twisted mushroom cloud roiled upward over the rock, blown away by the stiff wind.

"Of course we're far enough away," Flo said, her voice full of mockery. "Got any more brilliant ideas, oh master of stealth and subtlety?"

He shrugged. "Walk back and see what we uncovered, I guess."

The base of Ayers Rock looked like an ant hill that had just been kicked. The blast had carved a crater fifty feet deep into the base of it, exposing level after level of subterranean chambers and corridors. Even the Rock itself had been riddled with tunnels, but everything was choked with debris now. Workers were already busy clearing it aside, and warriors were taking up positions to defend the suddenly opened hole in their warren.

Fortunately there was also plenty of rubble on the surface to hide behind. Wang and Flo watched from behind a boulder at the lip of the crater while Exo's minions got to work repairing the damage. All of them wore hooded gray cloaks—apparently that was the uniform of Exo's service—but many of them walked with peculiar gaits that Wang recognized. Dog trots. Cat prances. Gator shuffles.

"Arrgh, beast men," he growled. "I *hate* beast men."

Flo shot him a pained look. "You're all beasts of one sort or another."

"True," Wang admitted. "But I learned how to fight human beasts. Screaming yellow platypus requires different form."

"Form won't make any difference against that many of them. We can't go in there."

Unfortunately, she was right. Wang knew his limits, and they fell somewhere short of the two hundred or so beast men that now patrolled the crater. Especially with a bullet hole in his left arm.

Direct assault wasn't his only weapon, however. Ninja were trained to slip past any guard, to penetrate any defense by stealth rather than by force if necessary. Left to himself, Wang could probably sneak right through the midst of everyone in that crater, but the problem was Flo. She was good with a .38 and with a four-inch cannon, but she hadn't learned how to disappear, and there wasn't time to teach her now.

Wang considered leaving her here while he went on, but he hadn't been lying to her on the airplane: he needed her to follow behind as insurance in case he was overwhelmed.

He shook his head sadly. "If we just knew where back door was, we could stroll in like we owned whole place. Guards are all *here*."

"Why don't we ask directions?"

"What?"

She laughed. "Men never think of that. Why don't we just stop someone and ask them where the back door is?"

"Oh," Wang said. "You mean capture them and torture information out of them. That could work, if we could get one or two of them alone."

"That's easy. Here." She stood up and waved down into the crater. "Yoo hoo! Hello down there!"

"What you doing? Get back here!" Wang grabbed her arm and yanked her back behind the rock, but it was too late. She'd been seen.

Chapter 17

Half a dozen beast men rushed through the rubble toward them. Flo said, "Trust me," and stood up and waved again. "Hi!" she said as they clambered up the crater rim. Putting on a Southern U.S. accent, she said, "Sorry to bother y'all, but I was on a tour bus when the meteor hit, and I got separated from the group. I think they left without me. I didn't know what to do until I saw you down here. I didn't even know there *was* an underground tourist center. Could I get somebody to tell me how to get down there? I'm afraid I can't climb through all this loose rock."

The one in front—a goat-man by the way he leaped so nimbly over the rocks—had his gun drawn, a big-bore automatic of some sort, but when Flo stood her ground and batted her eyelashes innocently at him he stopped a few paces away and lowered his weapon.

"No tourist center," he said. "This is . . . private facility."

151

"Oh," she said disappointedly. "But I'm lost, and—" she hesitated, as if embarrassed. "And I've got to pee."

Wang, hiding behind the rock, had to stifle a laugh. Too bad she didn't have a little camera with the motorized lens that stuck out like an obscene erection. Her lost-tourist story would be impossible to doubt if she had that.

The goat-man clearly didn't know what to do in this situation. "I can't let you in," he said. "Sorry. Private."

"But—but I'm lost!"

The other five beast men clambered up the slope, puffing hard. Wang, peeking out around the edge of the rock, saw that they carried long swords and had heavy shields slung across their backs. Or—wait. Were they shields? Yes, they had to be, but they looked biological. Part of the creatures themselves. Their chests seemed flat and hard as well. Their faces were wrinkled and leathery, and their fingers ended in sharp, curved claws.

These were the most animal-like creatures Wang had seen yet. Whatever bizarre genetic experimentation Exo was doing, this was too strange. All six of the beast men wore loose gray cloaks, so it was hard to tell what other odd mutations they sported, but what he could see was odd enough for Wang.

He tried to imagine the fighting form he would have to use against them. Turtles ducked for cover, swam deep, held their breath—and occasionally snapped with lightning speed. Yes. He had it now. He motioned to Flo to back away from the crater.

She nodded almost imperceptibly. "Let me get my

purse, and I'll be right back," she said, stepping backwards past the rock Wang crouched behind.

"Do not move!" ordered the goat-man. "Warhol, Pollock, go look for this woman's purse." Two of the turtle men moved to obey.

Just then, Flo caught her heel on a rock and fell backward. "Ow!" she yelled, grabbing her foot. "My ankle!"

Of course Warhol and Pollock had their eyes on her when they passed the spot where Wang hid. He waited for them to go past, then sprang out from behind and plucked their swords from their hands before they even knew he was there. They whirled around, but he dodged between them as they turned outward and he dived for cover behind another rock just beyond where Flo lay. He landed on his injured arm, but he didn't cry out.

"What was that?" asked one. They hadn't even seen him.

"What was what?" asked the goat-man.

"Something snatched our swords. Whistler, did you see anything?"

"Nothing," one of the others replied. "Picasso?"

"I thought maybe for a moment I saw the back and the front of an Asian man all at once, but that can't be so. My eyes had to be playing tricks on me."

"Well, something happened! Our swords are gone!"

While they discussed the situation, Wang crept along the back side of the rock he had jumped behind until he was only a foot or so from Flo's head. "Ancient Japanese saying," he whispered to her. "Suddenly a Wang shot out."

She snorted, then coughed to hide her laughter. He

whispered, "Sit tight. Wang take care of rest." He backed away and slipped behind another rock farther on, then peeked back to see the six beast men standing there scratching their heads.

"What did you do with their swords?" the goat-man demanded of Flo.

"I didn't do anything with their swords," she said. "But I think I sprained my ankle." She laughed again, but managed to turn it into a wail. "Oh—oh *spit!* It hurts."

The goat-man rolled his eyes. "See to her," he told the swordless duo. "The rest of you, split up and search the area." He marched past Flo and looked around the rock that Wang had just been crouching behind. The others moved away to the right and the left.

The debris field was dense enough and the boulders big enough that the searchers soon disappeared from sight. Wang listened carefully for footsteps, and by the clicking of hard hooves on gravel he knew that the goat-man was coming straight for his hiding place. He waited until he saw the barrel of a gun sticking around the edge of the rock, then lashed out with a foot and knocked it away in a kick so fast that two brittle hoof-like fingers went with it.

The goat-man was too surprised to yell. Using the goat form of fighting, Wang leaped up and butted him in the head with his own, knocking him cold. He pulled the unconscious beast man down and dragged him into cover, then checked his breathing. Still alive, but he would be out for a while.

The others hadn't noticed that their leader was missing yet. Wang moved toward the next one, sliding like a shadow between rocks, tossing pebbles to distract the turtle-man's attention at just the right moment, until he was able to reach out and pull the legs out from under his quarry.

The sound of his "Oof!" when he hit the ground with a thud and a rattle of his bony shield identified him as Whistler. Wang didn't have to knock him unconscious; he gagged him with a strip of cloth torn from the hem of his own cloak, bound his hands and feet together across his hard-shelled stomach, and left him on his back in the dirt.

Four to go. Wang stalked the next one, Picasso, and got him in a choke hold when he bent down to look at a caltrop that suddenly appeared at his feet. He left him trussed up like Whistler, and went for the next.

Warhol and Pollock were still helping Flo, completely unaware that their companions had been captured. The lone remaining turtle-man was moving warily, sword at the ready and eyes wide open as he poked through the debris for whatever mysterious force he was dealing with. Wang slipped from rock to rock, making bird calls and tossing pebbles to direct him into ambush.

At last the moment was right. Wang leaped out from a crevice in a split boulder as the beast man walked past and pinched the nerve at the creature's neck that should have numbed his entire sword arm, but he had forgotten one crucial detail: Turtles' nerves don't run along the same paths as humans'.

The turtle-man whirled around, sword already slashing toward Wang, and in that instant of clarity before he reached out and caught the sword arm he saw that this one was a turtle-woman. An old one, with a face even more wrinkled than the others' and a pair of round spectacles over her eyes.

"Exo's retirement plan must really suck," Wang said.

"Let go of me, you big oaf!" she cried out, kicking him and beating on his chest with her free arm.

"I am Lo Wang, not Big Oaf," he replied, forcing her arm back and squeezing her wrist until she dropped her sword.

Warhol and Pollock had heard her cry. "Grandma?" they called out.

"Over here!"

Wang gathered both her arms in his left hand and clapped his right hand over her mouth, but not before she screamed, "Help!" She kept struggling and kicking, and suddenly Wang felt knobby teeth sink into his index finger.

"Ow!" he exclaimed, yanking it away. "That's my trigger finger!" Blood welled up in an arc in the fleshy part at the base of it.

"I'll give you worse than that," she promised, but Wang ripped off the sleeve of her cloak and gagged her with it, then he tied her arms and left her struggling on her back like Whistler and Picasso. He ripped off another chunk of cloak and bandaged his finger with it.

He expected Warhol and Pollock to show up at any moment, but when thirty seconds or more passed without any sign of them, Wang peered cautiously around the edge of the rock and saw them standing next to Flo with their arms in the air. She held her chrome .38 trained on them.

"Very good," Wang said. "Come, join party." He

gathered up the four beast men he had captured, and used strips of cloth to tie and gag the goat-man as well as the others. He took Whistler's and Picasso's cloaks off before he bound them, and gave one to Flo.

"What's this for?" she asked.

"Camouflage," he said. "Here's plan: Now that we created diversion here with our nuclear explosion, we go for back door. It not heavily guarded now that action is here. With these cloaks we pretend to be Exo's underlings and walk right in. Then, we—"

"But we don't know where the—oops."

Wang scowled. She had blown it. He'd been trying to make the captives think he knew where he was going, so when they freed themselves they would lead him to the back door when they ran to help defend it. He thought furiously, trying to figure a way to salvage the situation. How could he turn her slip into an advantage?

They would have to pretend it wasn't a slip. Yes, that might work. In fact, maybe she had just handed him the perfect weapon. Wang smacked his head theatrically. "Oh, we don't know where back door *is*. Yes, of course. Silly me. Well, then, we will have to make one of these beast warriors lead us there." He bent down as if to untie Picasso, then paused. "On second thought, now that they know we don't know where back door is, they could simply refuse to divulge information, and Exo will be safe."

"I thought you were going to torture it out of them."

"We could try, but these trained ninja warriors. Very brave. It take long time to make one of them crack, if could be done at all." Wang stood up and rubbed his beard. "Hmm. No, we need make them think we already know where door is, then leave them tied up while we go hide somewhere and wait for them to loosen bonds. Then they have to run for back door themselves to warn guards we come, and we follow them there." He grinned. "What you think? It good plan, neh?"

Flo looked at him as if he'd just handed his sword to a mortal enemy. "It would have been great, but now they know we *don't* know, so it won't work."

Wang looked down at the six beast men, five turtles and a goat who had finally awakened again, all lying on their backs and listening intently. "No," he said, "plan will work, because they no can afford to believe us. We could lie when we say we don't know where back door is. Instead of hiding and waiting for them, we could just slip away and run straight for it. So they have to run for door too, just in case they can beat us there and block it against us."

"But if we're not lying . . ." She furrowed her brow.

"Why would we tell them something that harms us?" Wang asked. "Here, help me make sure they can get loose quickly—I not want to wait long for them to lead us to door." He tugged at the knots he had tied, loosening them up.

"You're crazy," Flo said.

"Yes, that is possibility, too." Wang laughed maniacally. "See, not even you know if I am telling truth. How can they do better?" He stood up and took her hand. "Come on, let's go hide. Or run for door. Oh, I can't decide what to do. Do you have coin to flip?"

He led her away before she could actually dig into her pocket.

"You can't think this will work," she whispered furiously at him.

"Of course it will," Wang replied. "I thought of it." He detoured around near the crater entrance to pick up his bag, but instead of carrying it he loaded the last of the ammunition onto his belt to replace what he had already fired, and he hung the pocket nuke from a grenade ring. He found walking a bit awkward when festooned with all that weaponry, but not as awkward as carrying a duffel bag in a fight. He tied the cloak tight around his waist with its rope belt and that helped hold down the load.

"Good, now we listen in," he said, leading the way back to a boulder not far from where they had left the beast men tied up. The wind made it hard to hear, but he caught a few words. Good; they had untied and ungagged themselves already.

". . . think he's right," said Picasso. "We can't afford to believe him."

"You mean not believe him," said Whistler.

"I mean we can't risk . . . without warning."

"Why don't we . . . the pit and . . ." the goat-man said.

"Because the corridors are choked with debris for . . . in every direction, that's why."

"I think some of us should . . . while the others go spread the warning," said the old woman. "If we see them following you . . ."

"And what's to prevent them from just tying you up again?" asked Pollock.

"We were surprised. Now we know. . . ."

"Like that's going to matter. No, we have to . . . for the door, just like they . . ."

Wang laughed softly. "I rest case," he said. "Come on." He led the way farther out into the rocks where they could follow without being spotted. It took a few more minutes for the beast men to make up their minds, and when they did it was obvious they had come up with a plan of their own. They had split into two groups, three of them going one way around the crater, the other three going the other.

"Which ones do we follow, Mr. Puzzle?" asked Flo.

"The ones in hurry, of course," said Wang. "See, group on the left has goat. Group on right has *old* goat. They are obviously diversion. We go left."

The beast men started running. It was all Wang and Flo could do to keep up with them and not be seen, but the nuclear explosion had blown a lot of debris out onto the plain. They stayed within a hundred yards or so, which was close enough. At least Wang hoped it was.

Suddenly the beast men swerved toward a small cave in the side of the Rock.

"That's it," Flo said, standing up from cover and pulling her revolver.

Wang yanked her back into hiding. "No, wait," he said. "In fact, we move on little bit."

"What? You really are nuts, aren't you? That's the doorway. If we let them make it, they'll be ready for us."

"And if we move on, we ready for them," said Wang.

He didn't wait for a reply. He flitted from boulder to boulder until he saw another cave a few hundred feet farther on. He led the way closer until they were within a few yards of it, then they crouched down to wait. Sure enough, in a few minutes here came the beast men, the two turtle-men puffing and panting far behind while the goat ran out ahead.

"It was another diversion," Flo said. "They were trying to smoke us out and I almost went for it."

"They have their own tricks," Wang said. "Fortunately, mine better than theirs. Let us see if this is right doorway." He took a shuriken from his belt and flung it at the goat-man. It buried itself in his neck, and he tripped and crashed to the ground.

"They're here!" shouted one of the turtle-men. "Quick, go warn the others; I'll hold them!" He drew his sword and rushed toward Wang. The other made a dash for the cave. It looked to Wang like he was running for real.

"Yes, now," he told Flo, standing up and pulling an Uzi from its holster.

Her .38 popped once. The Uzi spat fire. Both turtles dropped in their tracks.

"Time to ring doorbell," Wang said, blowing the smoke from the barrel of his gun.

Chapter 18

The cave looked natural for about thirty feet in. Wang was beginning to wonder if he had made a mistake, but just as it started to get dark enough that he worried about hitting his head on an overhang, he put out his hand and felt smooth metal overhead. Another few steps and their feet encountered concrete.

A spotlight came on overhead. Wang looked up and saw a motion detector beside it. It turned off when they passed, and another one turned on a few yards farther in. They walked along under the moving pool of light, and eventually came to a heavy metal door. Wang pulled on the wide lever and it swung noiselessly outward on oiled hinges.

A dog-man waited inside with an AK-47 held at the ready. Of course it would be a dog-man, Wang thought. Behind him a circular stairway and an elevator led farther into the complex.

"Password?" the guard asked.

"Pangaea," Wang said quickly, taking a wild guess.

"Wrong."

Wang scratched his beard. "You sure? I could have sworn it was pangaea."

"No."

"Must have been pangaea yesterday." He turned to Flo. "Was that yesterday? I lose track of time out on patrol." Without waiting for an answer, he turned back to the guard. "What day is today, anyway?"

"Friday," said the dog-man. He held his weapon pointed at Wang's stomach.

"No, can't be. It was Wednesday when we went out. We not been out two days, have we?" He scratched at the dried blood on his chest from the wound the tank gunner had given him.

Flo shrugged, finally getting into the act. "Could have been, I guess," she said. "It certainly feels like it."

"Well, if that's case, we were never *given* today's password. Pangaea have to do."

"It never *was* pangaea," said the dog-man.

"You're kidding."

"I don't kid."

Wang shrugged. "Your loss. Life without sense of humor is senseless life." In less time than it takes to blink, he reached out with his right hand and struck the gun barrel a sideways blow that not only deflected it from his stomach, but bent the barrel.

The dog-man pulled the trigger anyway. At full-auto the gun exploded in his hands and the breech blew backward into his own stomach.

"Good dog," Wang said. "That's just what Wang wanted you to do. Now sit."

The dog-man was no longer listening to him, but his legs gave out just as Wang spoke, and he fell to his knees.

"Roll over," said Wang, and the guard fell to his side.

"Play dead."

Flo looked down at the guard's body. "I don't think he's playing."

"No, I not think so either." Wang stepped over the body and looked down the circular stairwell. "All right, this where we split up. I go down and work my way toward command center. You wait ten minutes and follow. Take same path if you can; otherwise make your own."

"How will I know where you've been?"

He chuckled menacingly. "Look for bodies."

"I still want to go with you," she said.

"I know, but can't risk it. If I not get Exo, it's up to you." He handed her one of his Uzis.

She took a deep breath, and her breasts strained the confines of her clothing. Wang smiled. "Relax. Like you say earlier, piece of cake. When this all over we go back to France or Spain or somewhere warm and spend whole week making love on the beach."

"Right." She didn't sound convinced.

He leaned forward and kissed her. "Good luck."

"Luck," she said.

He turned away and started down the stairs. His footsteps echoed ahead of him. He thought he heard Flo say something more, but he couldn't be sure.

* * *

He had forgotten what silence sounded like. After hours of howling wind and roaring around in a tank, the interior of the underground complex seemed quiet as a tomb. Wang hoped it wouldn't become *his* tomb. He hated situations like this, walking blind into an enemy stronghold without even a glimmer of an idea where he was going. There were no You Are Here directories to help him get his bearings, no telephone booths where he could check a street map—he couldn't even climb up on something and look down. The place was well lit with fluorescent fixtures every few yards, but it was just a network of corridors hewn out of the rock with metal doorways leading into gloomy, low-ceilinged rooms, mostly empty now that everyone was helping clear the rubble from the bomb blast.

Mostly, but not quite. Wang surprised someone at work when he peeked into a laboratory of some kind. There were flasks full of red and brown fluid, with hoses and pipes connecting them to machinery that pinged and beeped and blinked. Vertical tanks along the far wall held humanoid shapes. Wang frowned when he saw them. This had to be where the beast man research went on. Probably just one of hundreds of such laboratories, considering how many beast men Exo employed, but Wang decided to cut the number by one.

The technician was a woman. Mid forties, heavy set, short blond hair going to gray. She looked a little like a cocker spaniel, Wang thought, but it was just the way she had pulled her hair back in little tufts over her ears. If she'd had dog genes she'd have been prettier. "Delivery," he told her when she looked up and saw him in the doorway. "Don't get up; I toss it to you." He unclipped a sticky bomb from his belt and armed it for close proximity, then lobbed it gently across the room toward her. He closed the door while it was still in the air and moved down the hallway a few feet. A muffled blast came from the laboratory, followed by a great crash of glassware and incubation tanks. A moment later, red fluid seeped out under the door and made a crescent in the hallway.

Wang dipped a finger in the stuff. It wasn't blood, but it was sticky and bright red so he used it to draw a crude yin-yang on the silver metal door. "My old Wang sign," he mused happily as he colored half the symbol in with blood. It dripped, but he didn't care. If Flo came this way, she would know he had been here.

He drew his remaining Uzi and went on, moving fast. The vibration of the ground told him that Australia was still on the move. No time for careful reconnaisance; it was time to rock.

He turned a corner and nearly collided with a wizened old man carrying a big box labeled TNT. Wang jumped back around the corner just as the geezer touched it off; the blast shook the corridor and blew debris against the walls to rain down on Wang. He shook his head and went around the corner again, only to find a floating specter of some sort where the TNT guy had been. He blasted it at point blank and was gratified to watch it shrivel and die, but he wondered if it was the bullets or the muzzle flash that had done it in. It looked suspiciously like the shadow creature Wang had fought back in Zilla's audience chamber.

So Exo was working with the forces of darkness as well, either on his own or through Zilla. It wouldn't surprise him to find out that the two were working together; they certainly had the same approach to attaining their goals. So long as their goals were compatible there would be no problem, but God help Exo if Zilla ever thought he was getting in the way.

Of course Exo wouldn't be around much longer to worry about that, not if Wang had anything to do with things. He stepped over the blackened spot on the floor where the hybrid monster had been and continued on down the corridor.

He was following his hunches more than anything in particular. Whenever he came to a cross-corridor he would sniff and listen and look to see which branch seemed more frequently used, or more opulent, or simply different in some way from the anonymous tunnels that made up the rest of the warren. When he came to stairways he invariably went down, though. He was willing to bet that Exo would set up his control center in the deepest, most heavily shielded place he could. When Australia met the other continents, he would need the most solid bunker in the world to ride out the collision.

True to his promise to Flo, Wang left a steady trail of bodies for her to follow. Twice more he had to shoot the spectral remains of enemies after he had blown up their physical bodies. He didn't like that; it made him twitchy to think enemies could come back for another go at him.

Then he laughed. That was no doubt how Zilla felt, too. He had almost certainly thought Wang was dead after the neurotoxin attack; what a surprise it must have been for him when Wang showed up again. No wonder he had retaliated so ruthlessly.

He blew up another lab—this one with dozens of techs and four newly hatched monsters that looked like failed attempts to clone ostrich-men. And in a corridor that widened out to the size of a city street, he encountered a seven-foot-tall, muscular beast that didn't look like it had been cloned from anything Wang had ever seen before. It was green and scaly and its body was all muscle, but it bulged in the wrong places. Its head was the size of a watermelon with a single top-knot of greasy black hair tied into a queue, its mouth held long curved fangs, and when it roared a challenge, it spewed red fire a good ten feet.

"Holy shit," Wang whispered when he saw it advancing on him. This hadn't come from any genetics lab he could imagine. This was pure, one hundred percent otherworldly.

The Uzi had no effect on it. Wang ducked into cover and pulled his four-barreled riot gun from its leg sheath, jumped back out, and let the creature have all four barrels. It howled and clawed at the bright red wounds that blossomed on its scaly body, but it didn't go down.

Wang lowered the gun, pulled his sword, and leaped forward. "Banzai!" he screamed, putting all his weight behind the blade as he brought it around in an arc that intersected the creature's neck. He felt a solid *chunk,* and the blade stuck about two-thirds of the way through like a saw bound in a tree limb. The creature howled again and spit more fire, some of which leaked out through the gash Wang had made in its neck. The rest would have scorched Wang's head from his shoulders if he hadn't ducked and rolled.

He came up shooting. Four more shotgun loads spun the creature around, and Wang leaped for his sword as the handle swung past. He wrenched it free from the smoking neck and hacked at it again, and this time the head fell free. It hit the ground and rolled under the creature's feet. Amazingly, the otherworldly beast was still standing, but it took a step and stood on its own head, and with a surprised flailing of arms it crashed to the floor. Wang rushed up and punctured it in the chest with his sword, stabbing the creature again and again until it shuddered and fell back limp.

It didn't keep its brain in its head. Either that or it had a spare in its abdomen. What was this thing? Wang picked up the head by its pointy green ears and examined it. Two little red eyes, a nose like a toad glued under the eyes, and that amazing gash of a fire-breathing mouth. How did it *do* that? He poked and prodded with a finger, feeling around the neck and ears and eyes for embedded hardware, but instead of an explanation he found the firing mechanism. Bright red flame shot out and sprayed off the wall beside him when he stuck his finger in one of its eye sockets. He gingerly held the head out so the mouth pointed away from him and stuck his finger in the other socket. Blue flame, more like an electrical discharge than fire, lanced out for at least thirty feet.

"Holy *pieces* of shit," Wang said. This could come in handy. He marched on down the corridor, whistling softly.

Chapter 19

He didn't even have to shoot the next couple of creatures he came across. The sight of him advancing on them with the head swinging from his fist was more than they could take; one fled screaming into the distance, while the other merely pulled its gun and blew its own head off the moment it realized what it was seeing.

"You smartest one here," Wang told the corpse as he stepped around the mess it had made. "Except me, of course."

The corridor seemed to go on forever. Wang stopped at the next junction he came to and looked for any clue to which direction he should go from here, but if there were any clues they weren't the kind he could recognize. If his sense of direction was still functioning in all these tunnels then he must be about in the middle of Ayers Rock by now, and fifty or a hundred feet beneath it, but that was just a guess.

That probably wasn't far enough down. The blast crater at the edge of the rock had exposed tunnels at least that far down; in the middle like this they would be deeper still.

There was an elevator a few hundred feet on down the corridor, but Wang kept walking. He didn't want to take an elevator; it would be too easy to get trapped in one. Stairs were much better.

He didn't find any near the elevator. Bad design. What if there was a fire? Then he laughed. If there was a fire this deep in an underground facility, everybody would be running for the exits on the perimeter, not heading up into the middle of the rock.

Hmm, Wang thought. That would be a good idea, actually. Now that he was in the middle, it would be great if everyone ran away from him.

But what about Flo? How far along was she? It had been at least fifteen minutes since Wang had started down. She would have jumped the gun by a few minutes, and he had fought his way through places she could merely walk through; she shouldn't be far behind, actually.

He walked back to the elevator. Sure enough, like practically any building anywhere, there was a red-handled fire alarm on the wall opposite the call buttons, with a big sign that said, "In case of fire, do not use elevator." Wang tapped the glass with the tiny hammer that hung on its chain beside the alarm, then reached inside and pulled the handle.

Just as bells began ringing all through the complex, a vial of bright purple dye burst open, spraying his hand with indelible ink. Wang looked at his marked hand and began laughing. "Caught in the act!" he said. "I did it! Oh, I'm very bad man. There will no doubt be big penalty for this."

Over the clamor of the alarm bells he heard the sound of many feet running. Wang moved on down the corridor until he found a stairway, used the fire-beast's blood to mark another yin-yang symbol beside the stairwell for Flo, then descended a few levels. Cloaked beast men hustled past, but Wang hid the grisly fire-breathing head under his own cloak and passed unnoticed in the confusion.

The air grew warmer the deeper he went. Wang paused to wipe the sweat from his brow. By the vibration and the smell of oil and hot grease, there were large machines nearby. Power generators, perhaps, or big pumps. Wang supposed a place this deep would need pumps to keep the ground water level low enough that it wouldn't flood. That might be a good way to stop Exo's plan—blow up the pumps—but again that presupposed he had a day or longer for the damage to take effect.

And if they were power generators? That would shut Exo down right away, wouldn't it?

Wang thought it over. It might, provided Exo didn't have any other power stations or backup batteries. That would be pretty stupid, though, and Exo wasn't stupid. More likely what would happen if Wang blew up a generator would be that he would lose his light here in this endless maze of corridors, and Exo would continue on his merry way without hindrance somewhere below.

That wouldn't be such a bad thing, actually. Wang had a pair of night-vision goggles in a pocket somewhere, if they hadn't gotten lost or crushed in all the fighting he had done. If he could see when Exo's strongarm force couldn't, that would be a decided advantage. He patted his weapons belt and pants pockets, and finally came up with the goggles. Still intact, by the looks of them. He slipped them on.

The corridor took on a greenish glow. Much too bright at the moment, but that was good. That meant they were working. Wang set off toward the source of the noise.

They were generators, all right. Geothermal ones, apparently, for Wang saw no sign of combustion engines, fuel tanks, or any provision to vent exhaust out of the immense cavern that housed the three enormous cylindrical hulks of metal. The generators themselves were silent, massive turbines balanced to within a feather's weight of perfection. Wang sensed their motion indirectly, the same way he sensed an enemy's motion before they knew themselves that they were going to move. It was all the support machinery, the transformers and cooling pumps and steam pipes, that made the rumble he had felt in the corridor outside.

He stood at a railing near the top of the generator cavern, looking down thirty or forty feet to the main floor. There were a few technicians down there checking gauges and polishing fixtures, but no guards. Wang looked around for the most vulnerable equipment, decided it had to be the big transformers beside each generator. Without those, electricity wouldn't go anywhere. How best to take them out, though?

Electrical things usually responded poorly to short circuits. He wondered if he could short those transformers out from here. They were encased in metal boxes, but they didn't look particularly well armored. If he could punch a hole through their cases and shove a metal rod into their interiors, he bet that would do the trick.

Wang smiled. That he could do from here. He set down the bloody beast head and drew his rail gun, the electromagnetic slug launcher. He aimed for the center of the transformer at the far end of the cavern. There was a soft zipping sound when he pulled the trigger, and a tiny hole appeared in the casing. Bright blue sparks immediately shot out the hole. The overhead lights flickered, but didn't go out.

Wang shot the second transformer. More sparks, and this time a loud screech as the turbine lurched against its mooring under the sudden change in load.

Technicians rushed for the transformers. Wang calmly shot the third one.

The lights went out immediately, but he didn't need to slide his night-vision goggles down over his eyes just yet. Sparks continued to fly as the turbines kept providing power. It looked like the welding section of an automobile assembly line down there; bright flashes that lit up the scene with stroboscopic clarity.

The second turbine had mangled its bearings when it made its sideways lurch. The massive generator banged back and forth within its cradle, then with a roar of overstressed metal and a hiss of superhot steam, it finally ripped itself apart and spewed metal fragments the size of people throughout the cavern. Wang, on his catwalk above the generators, watched the steam and sparks and flying chunks of metal with delight. Exo wouldn't be getting power from here any time soon.

He holstered his rail gun, picked up the demon head, slipped his night-vision goggles down over his eyes, and headed back into the labyrinth.

Two nuclear blasts, a fire alarm, and a power outage had definitely stirred things up. Wang moved stealthily through the darkness, his amplified goggles displaying everything in shades of green. The enemy were easy to spot; their bodies were brighter than their surroundings and they moved slowly now, clumsily feeling their way along darkened corridors. Wang stayed clear of their groping hands, slipping among them as he worked his way ever downward. Occasionally he would slit the throat of a door guard and take a look at what he was guarding, but he found nothing useful.

At last he reached an area that people seemed to be rushing *toward,* even though they were still deep underground. This looked promising. Wang followed a group of four gray-cloaked beast men as they stumbled their way through the dark through ever-larger corridors, and they eventually came to a security door. There was an emergency light shining over the door, and Wang could see regular fluorescent light spilling out through the narrow window from beyond it. He had reached the self-contained command center.

The beast men he had followed there lined up and pressed their left hands against an electronic lock plate beside the door. Each one allowed the one in front of him to go through the door and then let the door close again before he repeated the procedure. There was evidently a warm-body counter as well as a coded lock to prevent anyone from slipping through without authorization.

Wang stepped up behind the last man in line just as the door closed in front of him. He quickly snapped the man's neck, caught him before he fell, then held his limp hand up to the lock. The door clicked, and Wang pulled the handle. No alarm.

He tossed the body back down the corridor into the darkness, slid off his goggles and pulled his hood up over his head, then stepped through the door.

This cavern was even bigger than the one that held the power generators. It was at least a couple of hundred feet across and fifty feet high, with massive floor-to-ceiling columns of rock to keep it from collapsing. It was decked out like a launch control center for a space mission. Rows of computer consoles set in semicircles faced an enormous situation board on the far wall, a twenty-by-thirty-foot flat monitor on which images of the continents were displayed. Beside that a ten-foot globe spun slowly, showing the same information in 3D. Wang took in the continents' positions as he sidled away from the group he had come in with. North and South America were nearly touching Europe and Africa. The Mediterranean Sea was just a narrow slit now. And Australia had plowed through most of Indonesia on its way toward the Arabian Sea.

Wang looked closer and realized that Australia hadn't actually run the islands down; they had been shifted northward to fill the Bay of Bengal and back up against Vietnam.

Dozens of arrows pointed the direction of motion

for each major landmass, and the arrows' size no doubt indicated relative velocity. Exo had done plenty of damage already, but it looked like the world had maybe half an hour, forty-five minutes at the outside, before the major continents started smashing into one another.

Wang felt sweat beading on his forehead. Part of it was his own metabolism, cranked up for battle, but part of it was the cavern itself. It was just plain hot this far underground.

All the same, Wang was glad for his hooded gray cloak. It gave him a chance to figure out the situation before he made his move, though even with the cloak it was hard to remain inconspicuous with a severed head and half a dozen assault weapons making odd bulges beneath the cloth. At least the head wasn't dripping blood anymore. Wang considered taking up a position in the center of the control room and turning its unnatural fire on everyone there, but there were forty or fifty computer operators, a dozen beast men with automatic weapons standing guard over them, and messengers running back and forth from console to console. Some of them were bound to survive the assault, and then it would degenerate into a firefight with Wang as the target.

He looked for other options. When he turned around and looked behind him he saw a glass wall above the door he had come in through, with still more people looking down into the control room from behind it. It was a good thing he hadn't attacked rashly; he would have had to take them out as well.

All the same, he had been standing still too long. Nothing sticks out in a bee hive more than a lazy bee.

Wang walked around the outer ring of computer consoles, trying to decide what to do. There was a table against the back wall with an urn of coffee and a tray of snacks on it. He stopped there to slake his thirst and eat something for energy. The stuff tasted as terrible as any institutional coffee and snacks, but it was better than nothing.

When he judged that he had monopolized the snack tray long enough, he continued walking around the room, looking over the hunched shoulders of their operators to see what they were working on. Most of it was just lists of numbers and meaningless graphs, but one screen showed something Wang recognized. It was the interior of a spaceship, and an alien monster was advancing with a double-bladed sword in either hand. He had played this game on one of the union guys' computers back in New York. "Unreal," Wang whispered.

The computer operator jerked as if he'd been slapped. He hit a couple of buttons and the game vanished, replaced by a smaller version of the 3D globe beside the situation board at the front of the room.

Wang stepped up behind him. "You're relieved," he said.

The operator turned to look at him. It was a woman, a cat-woman by the narrow cheekbones and the slit pupils of her eyes. She licked the back of her hand and ran it over her reddish yellow hair to paste down a stray curl of bangs. "Who, me?" the action seemed to ask.

"This is not time for games," Wang said. "If you must play, go do it somewhere else."

"I—I couldn't help myself," she said. "I was bored, and—"

"Yes, yes. Go. Find bird-man to chase, but leave now." He pulled her chair backward and lifted her out of it, then sat down and scooted in. She stood for a second behind him, but he pretended to ignore her. In truth, he was watching her reflection—and the reflections of all the guards and other computer operators behind him—in the monitor's shiny glass surface.

At last she shrugged and moved away. Wang watched until she went out through one of the doors in back—not the one he had entered through, he was glad to note. If she spotted the body he had left in the hallway, she would no doubt have raised the alarm.

It wouldn't be long before someone did just that. Wang turned his attention to the monitor. Perhaps he could simply shut down the ABCD device from here before anyone was the wiser.

Chapter 20

Computers were not his forte. He silently thanked the gods for graphic interfaces or he would never have figured it out. As it was it took him a couple of minutes to find a menu that looked promising, but even when he selected ABCD Functions he couldn't find a selection that would simply turn it off.

He explored the selections he had. Drift Rate looked promising, but it turned out to be just a passive display. Evidently that was controlled from another terminal. So what did this one control? Wang looked for a label on the monitor, but saw only a Dilbert cartoon taped to the edge. Apparently Exo's minions didn't like their workplace any more than anyone else did.

He noticed the brand name on the computer itself and smiled. Wang. "Good name," he said. He hoped it was a good omen, too.

His console had to control *something*. Wang selected Rotation off the menu and typed a string of eights into the blank labeled Degrees/hour, then pressed Execute. He felt a moment of dizziness, but it passed as quickly as it had come. He looked up at the situation board to see if anything moved.

He didn't spot it at first. He was watching Africa and Asia and the major continents for signs of motion, but it wasn't on the main board where the action happened. It was off to the side, where the 3D globe had suddenly begun to spin like a top.

"Ow!" Someone behind him shouted. Wang looked around and saw one of the technicians at the refreshment counter pouring himself a cup of coffee. At least that's what he was trying to do. The stream of coffee left the spout of the pot, but instead of falling into the cup it bent sideways.

"Coriolis force!" Wang muttered. Master Shoji had warned him to correct for it when he made a long throw with a shuriken, but Wang had never seen it this pronounced. He turned back to his console and quickly typed in 24, then backspaced over that and typed 15. The units were degrees per hour, not hours per day.

Another wave of dizziness passed over him, and the globe at the front of the room slowed down to normal. Wang realized everyone in the room was staring at him. He shrugged his shoulders and tugged his hood down farther over his face, belatedly remembering to lick his hand and rub his cheeks with the back of it.

People looked away, muttering and shaking their heads. Wang silently thanked the gods for the cat-woman, who must have had a reputation for such lapses.

The experience confirmed something Wang had suspected all along, though: The ABCD device had to use force fields of some sort to manipulate the continents. There was no way something like what he had just done could be accomplished without them. Direct force applied through motors or levers or anything like that would have turned the world to mush just now.

Man-animal clones, supernatural beings, and now force fields. Wang was getting a little tired of finding himself up against unfamiliar powers. Maybe now was the time to put a stop to it, even if he was outnumbered.

He had tried indirect methods and had not gotten anywhere. The continents were still rushing toward oblivion. "Ancient Japanese saying," Wang muttered. "If first you don't succeed, try bigger hammer."

He carefully eased a sticky bomb off of his weapons belt without letting it show from beneath his gray cloak. He stuck it to the underside of the computer desk and activated it as he stood up. The next person who sat there would get a big—if momentary— surprise.

Grasping the grisly head beneath the folds of the cloak, he walked over toward the door where he had come in, stopping a few paces short of it. This room wasn't a perfect ellipse like Zilla's audience chamber, but it was oblong, and Wang was now standing in one of the two spots where sound would be reflected from best.

He opened his cloak and pulled out the head.

Holding it by its hair with his left hand, he held the index finger of that same hand near its eyes. With his right hand he drew his Uzi. Then, putting all his voice into it, he yelled, *"Anybody want any Wang?"*

Half the people in the room jerked around and looked at him. The other half jerked around and looked at the spot where his voice reflected to.

Wang fired the Uzi at the guards who looked toward him. At the same time, he jabbed his finger into the head's left eye socket, and the crackling blue discharge flared out of its mouth into the room. Where it touched computers, they burst into showers of sparks. Where it touched people, they burst into showers of blood.

"Eat hot death, minions of evil!" he shouted. He had always wanted to yell that.

The guards who had looked the wrong way couldn't miss the flames roaring through the air. They whirled around and fired at Wang, but he didn't wait to be shot down. Still spraying the room with bullets and supernatural fire, he backed away, darting this way and that in the random, impossible-to-follow fashion of a Shadow Warrior. He directed his fire at the beast men with guns first, slamming them up against the stone wall with a hail of bullets or blowing them to bits with the demon head.

One of them got in a lucky shot. Wang felt a bullet smack into the head, and suddenly the blue flame flickered and died. Wang immediately blasted the guard with a burst from his Uzi, but it was too late for the head. He tried sticking his finger in its other eye, but instead of a rush of red fire it only vomited a sticky yellow goo that hissed and bubbled on the floor.

"That has always been problem with relying on head," Wang said sadly. "Much too fragile in fight." He flung the head upward in an arc over the middle of the room, drew his riot gun while it was still on the upswing, and fired a shot straight into it. The head exploded in a shower of blood and brains and unnatural burning gore that rained down on the people and computer consoles that Wang hadn't already destroyed.

Not bad. Ten seconds and half the people in the room were dead, plus the control center was in flames. Wang risked a look upward at the glass wall in back. He could see many people running around up there, but nobody had thought to break the glass and start shooting down at Wang yet. Good. He turned back to the rest of the room and fired his Uzi and the riot gun at anything that moved.

The person at the terminal next to the one Wang had booby-trapped fell forward with a bullet in his chest, but the moment he drew close enough to the sticky bomb under the desk it exploded and flipped what was left of him backward, knocking down the person behind him who was scrambling for cover behind yet another terminal. Wang blew up the computer first, then finished off the drone.

"Ooh, you should never have applied for terminal job," he said. "Bad career move."

No guards remained standing, and the ten or fifteen operators who were left had managed to duck behind their consoles. Wang lobbed a couple of grenades down into the center of the complex and watched as computer parts and operator parts flew outward from the explosions.

The enormous situation map at the front of the cavern flickered and went dark. The 3D globe lurched to a stop, its continents all on one side but not quite touching yet. Wang stopped shooting for a second to feel for vibration, hoping he might have stopped Exo's plan by ruining the control center, but the floor still rumbled with the deep subsonic grinding of a continent on the move. He had only smashed Exo's pretty toys; he hadn't touched the actual ABCD device they were connected to.

He looked again at the room behind the glass. He would bet money that Exo himself was up there. In fact, he would bet a billion dollars against his life that that was where the mastermind behind all this spent his time. That would be the perfect place to look down on the nerve center and watch his plans unfold. And that was where Wang needed to go if he wanted to stop those plans.

He looked for a stairway or an elevator into the observation room, but there was no obvious way up there. Of course there wouldn't be; a man like Exo couldn't even imply to his workers that there was a connection between him and them. The entrance to his private command center within the command center would be from behind or above.

Wang couldn't see as many figures moving around up there as he had seen before. He imagined that meant most of Exo's personal guards were on their way down the back stairs to kill the intruder. Now would be a good time to leave the cavern and find a way *up*.

Before he could reach the door, a speaker clicked on overhead and a howl of feedback filled the cavern. "Well, Mr. Wang," said Exo's amplified voice. "You're just in time to witness the re-creation of a supercontinent. Pity you ruined the display; I had some rather clever graphics programmed for the moment of contact. Which, by the way, should be about twenty minutes from now."

"I didn't come to watch pictures," Wang told him. "I came to collect on bet. I survived plane flight, you owe one billion dollars. Small unmarked bills will be fine."

"You couldn't carry a billion dollars in small bills," Exo said contemptuously. "That would weigh, let's see, three fourths of a gram times a billion, carry the seven—"

"I'll use forklift," Wang told him. "You have money?"

"What are you talking about? Of course I don't have a billion dollars. Do you have any idea how much it costs to keep an evil lair staffed and equipped? There's the tunneling machinery and the contractors to pay for, bribes to the local government, the staff. It doesn't just happen, you know. It all takes money. I've got a quarter million in doors alone. Sixty thousand in light switches, for Pete's sake. I've mortgaged myself to the hilt for this place, and I'm not giving what's left to you just because you made it here on your own steam. I'm just going to kill you, you idiot."

Wang pulled the last of his sticky bombs from his belt and listened carefully for the rush of many feet on stairs. The moment he heard that, he would make his move. Exo was obviously stalling while his elite troops got into place; well, two could play that game. Wang would stall until they were all downstairs, then make a quick exit. "Hmm. Sore loser," he said.

"I haven't lost!" Exo shouted. "Can't you get that through your head? You're right where I want you. You've walked into another trap."

"Then Lo Wang had better leap out of it," Wang said. He'd heard the first hint of echoing footsteps beyond the doors.

He tossed the sticky bomb gently upward so it came to rest on the glass wall. Nobody on the other side was stupid enough to come investigate and trigger the proximity fuse, but that didn't matter. Wang backed across the room and fired his Uzi at it, and the bomb exploded in a bright hail of glass fragments.

"Mmm," Wang said. "I love sound of breaking glass. Almost as good as sound your head will make when I crush it between my hands." Hooded shapes rushed forward from inside the room he had just exposed; he tossed a grenade through the shattered wall and ducked behind a computer console.

The blast echoed in the cavern, and the screams and barks and howls of wounded beast men followed on its heels. Then the doors on the ground level burst open and more beast men poured in like water from a fire hose.

He had waited too long. Wang leaped up from his cover, firing his Uzi in one hand and the riot gun in the other while he took three long steps, jumped to the top of the rearmost computer console, and sprang off the monitor with a forward roll that sent him high into the air and backward through the last of the glass fragments still standing in the overhead wall. He landed on a wounded lion-man and received a nasty gash on his right shoulder from the beast's claws before he rolled free and fired point-blank into its oversize head, but he was too busy to see if he'd finished the lion-man off.

The upper room was as big as the lower one, just set back a ways like the balcony section of an old theater. It had the same massive columns of stone to hold up the ceiling, the same rows of computer consoles, plus a central dais with a big leather swivel chair from which Dr. Exo could watch over the heart of his empire.

There was nobody in the chair. Exo had fled, probably the moment the sticky bomb had landed on the glass.

The upper control room didn't hold as many people as the lower one had, but the ones who were there were already on the alert. Bullets smacked into computers and more esoteric equipment as Exo's guards tried to eliminate the intruder who had suddenly appeared in their midst. Wang ducked behind whatever cover he could find—machinery, bodies, live beast men, it didn't matter—and fired back at anything that moved. He tried to spot Exo amidst the chaos of screaming enemies and flying bullets, but everyone wore the same stupid gray cloaks. Wang might have already killed him and never known it.

As long as he was dead. Wang fired a wild burst over his shoulder with the Uzi to force everyone else to take cover, then rose up again from behind the bank of electronic equipment where he had taken refuge and squeezed off a round with the riot gun.

Click. The gun was empty.

Chapter 21

He covered for his mistake with another burst from the Uzi while he dropped back down behind the console and frantically reloaded. Only four more shells. He would have to use them carefully.

The Uzi was about out as well. Wang turned and sprayed the last of its clip down into the lower control room, forcing the new arrivals down there to duck for cover, then he ejected the empty magazine and slid in a fresh one. That was his last for that, too; then he would be down to just the rail gun.

Exo might have more henchmen than Wang had bullets. Wang didn't like that thought. He pulled out his last two grenades and tossed one over the console into the upper gallery, and the other down into the lower control room, aiming for the thickest concentration of beast men. It made sense to use the weapons of mass destruction when there were masses of enemies to be destroyed, and save his bullets for the one-on-one mopping up.

The grenades exploded half a second apart. Wang heard howls and barks as the beast men reverted to form in their panic to escape the carnage. He rose up and sprayed bullets at the milling figures in the upper room with him, then ducked down and jumped for cover behind a different console before anyone could take aim at him.

The smell of gunpowder and blood was growing strong enough to make his breath catch in his throat. The air ventilation had evidently stopped when he'd blown the main power generators. The heat had become nearly unbearable now that he was fighting hard; he felt slick from his own sweat. He hoped he could finish everyone off soon, if for no other reason than so he could blow up the ABCD device and get back into some fresh, cool air.

He didn't even know what the device looked like. All he knew was that it was still working, still channeling energy from the Earth's core into the motion of the continents. How could he blow it up if he didn't know what it looked like?

The nuclear bomb riding at his hip would be one answer. Detonated down here, it would almost certainly take out the device. Unfortunately it would take Wang with it, because he couldn't afford to leave it on a timer. The chance that someone could find it and defuse it before it blew would be too great.

Where was Exo? It was starting to bug Wang that he didn't know. Exo had obviously been able to see Wang down below; that meant he'd been sitting in the command chair a minute ago.

Unless he'd been watching by remote camera. That could put him anywhere. But no, he had shut up the moment Wang had tossed his sticky bomb against the glass. No megalomaniac could resist the urge to threaten their enemy at a moment like that unless they were busy diving for cover.

One of the beast men who had survived the grenade was rallying the others for another attack. He seemed to be everywhere at once, nipping and snarling at the others and forcing them forward. A border-collie-man, by the look of it. Wang fired a burst from the Uzi at him, but the collie-man was fast; Wang had to follow him left and right as he ducked behind desks and electronics racks, popping out only long enough to shoot back at Wang and force *him* to duck and spoil his aim.

Then the collie-man made his fatal mistake. He ducked behind a computer console that stood by itself. Wang only needed to wait until he showed his head, then blow it off.

He fired a few more bullets from the Uzi to keep everyone else down, but after three shots the Uzi clicked empty. "Sonofabeech!" Wang cursed, dropping the useless weapon and raising the riot gun. This was taking too long!

Boom, the first shot shattered the computer the collie-man ducked behind. *Boom,* the next one shredded the desk it had been sitting on. *Boom,* the third one blew the operator's chair to bits, filling the air with shredded foam rubber. The collie-man held his ground, his gun aimed directly at Wang. *Boom,* the fourth shot blasted him back against the wall, but not before he got off a shot of his own. Wang felt the impact at his hip, felt a crackling jolt of electricity, and frantically struck at the source of it: his electro-magnetic rail gun, its case shattered and its battery now discharging all at once through his body.

He knocked the rail gun from his belt and it clattered to the floor, still sparking and smoking. Wang kicked it down into the lower gallery, scattering the beast men who had just begun to rally again after the last grenade. That was the last of his Western weapons, though; now he was down to sword and shuriken. And a nuke, if things got grim, but he wasn't anywhere near that point yet.

It was hard to tell, with everyone hiding from him, but he guessed there were maybe ten people left alive in the upper control room, and twenty or so below. Not good odds. He picked up a handful of plastic debris from the floor and flung it piece by piece with quick snaps of his wrist so it smacked hard into the places where he knew enemies were hiding. Maybe it would keep them down so he could take them on one at a time.

He drew his sword and moved toward the closest one, trying to remember everything Master Shoji had taught him—everything *anyone* had taught him—at once. *Kay equals one half em vee squared. Walk softly and carry a big stick. Wash colors separately.*

He heard a squeak and a scurrying sound from behind a floor-to-ceiling column. Rats? More like a rat-man; it was a big squeak. A rat-man afraid for his life, most likely, so he would no doubt fight like a cornered rat. That is to say, he would leap out the moment Wang got too close, all teeth and claws in Wang's face.

Wang readied his sword, then stuck his foot around the edge of the column.

Sure enough, the rat-man screeched and jumped out at him—and impaled himself directly on the point of Wang's sword. Wang yanked it out of his chest and swept the blade sideways and back again, neatly slicing off the creature's head. He grabbed it before it could roll away and lobbed it down into the lower gallery, where it struck with a wet thunk like a watermelon falling from a shopping cart. Maybe that would discourage anyone who was wondering if they should join the fight upstairs.

"Yes, you all stay in state of high Wanxiety, eh?" he said.

He laced three of his star-shaped shuriken between his fingers, then crept around the column where the rat-man had just died. Bullets ricocheted off the stone just over his head. Wang could tell it wasn't one of the original guards firing the gun; the first shot was the only one even close before the gun's recoil made the rest of the clip go wild. Wang waited for the panicked gunman to run out of bullets, then he rose up and threw the shuriken at him. The poor guy looked like a gerbil-man or a hamster-man, pudgy cheek pouches quivering with nervousness, but then the shuriken hit him and he fell to the floor like any other dead man.

Everyone else had ducked down again, so Wang pressed the attack. He slashed the air with his sword until it shrieked and he jumped up on a desk where he could see the cowering beast men, whom he chased down one by one. Some of them tried to fight, using uncommon forms adapted to their hybrid bodies, but

Wang adjusted to their styles and sliced his way through them.

The snake-man weaved from side to side and spit venom; Wang weaved right back at it, holding its attention with the gleaming tip of his sword until he could lash out and break its neck with the side of his hand.

The hippo-man roared a challenge and tried to crush Wang beneath his rubbery bulk, but Wang roared right back at him and stampeded him over the balcony edge, where he landed with a considerably wetter splat than the rat head had.

The rabbit-man kicked with the speed and power of lightning, but he had to turn his back to do so. Wang danced around him, always staying in front while he kicked and slashed at the creature's powerful legs from relative safety. He heard bone break, and the rabbit-man fell to the ground.

"You in hopeless situation, bunny," Wang told it, then he ended its misery with a quick slash of his sword.

The Tasmanian-devil-man came at him like a spinning top, its arms and legs and snapping teeth just a blur of motion. Wang spun around in the opposite direction, whipping his sword around even faster, and they collided like two saw blades ripping through the same board. Wang's sword proved harder than the devil-man's teeth and claws; its severed arms went flying out in centrifugally flung arcs, trailing streams of blood. A moment later its head bounced to the ground, and Wang kicked it down to land with the rat-man's head and the hippo-man.

Now that he was fighting hand to hand, the wounds in his arm and chest were really starting to bother him. Even the finger wound from the turtle bite had started throbbing again. He had to finish this soon. Where was Flo, anyway? She should have made it here by now. With her backing him up, the two of them could end it right then and there.

Wang heard a whistle, then two more beast men came up from cover simultaneously. Wang sized up the situation immediately: a badger-man and a huge-clawed crab-man.

The badger-man struck first, snarling and lunging with his long snout full of sharp teeth. Wang swung his sword while he backed away and felt the blade bite into the beast man's side, but that only enraged it. *Bad move,* Wang thought. A wounded badger was even more dangerous than a healthy one.

Sure enough, the badger-man accelerated into a blur of teeth and claws. Wang felt the claws rake his chest, reopening the bullet wound there, and then the badger-man was inside his guard. A row of razor-sharp teeth clamped down on his sword arm. Wang kicked out with his left foot and caught the creature in the stomach, then grabbed his sword with his left hand and hacked at the black-and-white striped head. He felt the sword glance off bone, only enraging the badger-man further.

He heard a rustle of chitinous claws behind him and dropped just in time to avoid having his neck snipped in two by the crab-man's powerful pincers. The crab-man had sidled around behind him while the badger-man had kept him occupied. Wang braced himself and whirled around, pulling the badger-man around by his teeth, and slammed him sideways into the crab-man.

All three went down in a tumble of arms and legs. The badger-man pulled free of Wang's arm, but before he could attack again, Wang remembered his badger form and lunged for the creature's throat. He didn't have the teeth for it, but he made up for that in power and desperation; he felt the carotid arteries pulse beneath his teeth, then he bit down and felt the hot gush of blood splash out through the bite.

The badger-man fell back to the ground, air bubbling through the hole in his throat. Wang spit out the chunk of bloody flesh in his mouth and pushed himself to his feet.

The crab-man was already standing, sliding around sideways so he could get his claws into position again. Wang moved into a crab stance as well, circling sideways and holding his sword arm high. The crab-man lunged with his right claw and Wang leaped back just as it snapped shut where his head had been. Wang hacked at it with his sword, but the blade glanced off the hard chitin without causing any damage.

"Oooh, I get very crabby when that happens," Wang told him. He looked for a vulnerable spot, but this creature had kept far more of his animal genes than the usual beast man. He was covered in chitin from head to foot, and though he only had two legs, they were thick and knobby and ended in sharp claws.

One pincer was much bigger than the other. "High mass, slow velocity," Wang said, ducking beneath it before the crab-man could react. He jabbed his sword into the joint where arm met carapace, and felt it

198

punch through the relatively weak shell there. Wang rotated the sword, feeling it cut through muscle, then jumped back when the claw dropped toward him.

The claw kept going, falling limp to the creature's side. It nearly touched the floor. Wang could have cut it off easily now, but he left it attached. As dead weight it did Wang far more good slowing down his adversary.

The crab sidled around until the other claw was in position. Wang sidled around with it in perfect crab form, then faked like he was going to try the same maneuver on that side, but the crab-man was faster with the smaller claw and dropped it to protect the tender spot. As soon as it was committed to that motion, Wang swept the sword upward and slashed at the crab-man's tiny eyes, which protruded out on stalks from its forehead. The stalks were chitin too, but they couldn't hold back a sword; with a crack like twigs breaking, both eyes dropped to the floor and the creature was blind.

Wang froze in position with his sword raised. He stood perfectly silent for a second, two seconds, until the crab-man turned slightly to the right and raised its claw in preparation to strike at the first noise it heard. Unfortunately for it, the first noise it heard was Wang's sword entering its other armpit, and this time he leaned in and buried the blade all the way to the hilt before wiggling it around and stirring up the creature's insides.

The crab-man collapsed with a clatter of chitin. Wang pulled his sword free and turned to see what else he faced. There was only one more figure standing, a tall, slender, hooded creature of indeterminate ancestry who stood by a bank of electronic equipment against the back wall and watched the proceedings without apparent fear.

Wang knew who this one had to be. He turned to face him, wiped sweat from his eyes, and said, "Time to pay up."

"Not on your life," said Dr. Exo. His voice wasn't quite as deep in person, but it was impressively rich.

"That was general idea," Wang said, stepping toward him. He moved cautiously. Something wasn't right here. Exo was right by a door; he should have bolted for safety long before Wang finished off the last of his defenders.

Was he immobilized by fear? The air stank too badly of blood and gunpowder for Wang to tell by smell. There *was* an unusual aroma, something that set Wang's neck to tingling, but he couldn't identify it. He took another step closer.

"You turn off ABCD device, I let you live," he said.

"I have a better idea," said Exo. "You freeze right where you are and I let *you* live, at least long enough to witness my triumph."

Why did Exo sound so confident? He had lost all his guards and was about to lose his own life. Was this just last-minute bravado, or did he have a weapon up his sleeve? Wang examined his adversary closely. Exo stood with one hand poised in front of a rack of switches and dials. His other hand hung loose at his side. He didn't have the stance of a man who was about to attack.

Maybe Wang should just fling a shuriken into his brain and be done with it. The only trouble with that was he didn't know where the ABCD device was, or how to shut it off when he found it. He needed Exo to do that.

Unless the panel of electronic equipment beside him was the device. Maybe that's why Exo seemed so confident; maybe he could control everything from right there.

Even so, it was too late. He might be able to push a button or two before Wang could kill him, but that would be it. Wang could end his life with a single swing of his sword, then he could figure out what he had done and undo it while Exo bled at his feet.

He took another step.

Exo pushed a button.

Wang froze.

Chapter 22

An invisible force held him fast. Wang tried to raise his sword arm, but it felt as if the blade was buried in a tree. He couldn't even move his fingers to let go of it, nor could he move his other arm, hand, feet—nothing. Even the sweat had stopped dripping from his forehead. He could barely breathe. It was worse than being buried under rocks in the cave back in Spain. At least there he could tell what held him; here he felt as if he were embedded in glass.

"Once again I have managed to trap you just when you thought you had won," said Dr. Exo. "Such a pity. You were doing so well, too."

"It's not . . . over . . . yet," Wang managed to croak out with his frozen lips and tongue.

"Oh, but I do believe it is," said Exo. He lowered his hand and moved away from the electronics rack. "This is the same type of force field that the ABCD device uses to control the continents. I doubt if even the great Lo Wang will be able to break free of its grip. It's over for you, and in another few minutes it will be over for most of the world. The Americas are just about to collide with Europe and Africa, and when they do, that will be the end for humanity!" Exo rubbed his hands together gleefully.

"Why?" Wang asked. "What . . . you . . . accomplish?"

"Accomplish? Accomplish? Ridding the Earth of this vile pestilence isn't enough? Well then, think of it as a work of performance art if you'd rather."

Wang saw a motion behind Exo. In the window of the door, a face appeared. He tried not to let his expression betray any surprise—not an easy thing to do even with the force field holding him tight, because the face belonged to Flo.

"Your art . . . *sucks*," Wang told him, hoping to keep Exo's attention focused on his captive while Flo opened the door. "Should have peed in bottles . . . or burned flag . . . if you wanted . . . make real art."

His ploy worked. "Hah, what do you know about art, you cretin!" Exo screamed. He took another step toward Wang. "You wouldn't know good performance art if someone staged it on your forehead."

"Maybe not . . . but bad is . . . easy to recognize."

"Hah! I suppose you think—"

Flo opened the door. She had her chrome .38 out, aimed right at Exo. Wang was directly behind him, but he didn't care.

"Shoot him!" Wang yelled. He jabbed toward the master of evil with his sword, putting all his effort behind it, but only managed to move the blade an inch.

Exo whirled around, crouching low.

Flo's gun didn't move. It still pointed at Exo. "Are you all right?" she asked.

"Shoot!" Wang yelled.

"Why yes, thank you," said Exo. He straightened up and held out his hand. "And you, my dear? How was your trip?"

"Rough," she said, lowering her gun. "I had a hell of a time getting this musclebound oaf—"

"Flo!" Wang cried out. "What . . . you saying?"

"I'm saying you damned near got me killed half a dozen times, that's what!" She clenched her fists in cold rage. The .38 fired and a bullet ricocheted off the floor, glanced off a stone column, and buried itself in the massive leather chair atop the dais.

"Oops. Sorry, Father."

"Father?" Wang screamed. "You . . . he . . . impossible."

"Oh, it's possible all right." She stepped past Exo and stood next to Wang. She holstered her gun and held out her hands to him, stopping a foot or so away when she encountered the force field. "I took the place of the real Florelle Morgan at the same time Daddy kidnapped her mother. We knew the CIA would try to send someone after her, and they would come to me for information. It was easy to make sure I tagged along. I kept tabs on you, made sure you didn't get here soon enough to stop us. You were far more resourceful than we imagined, but ultimately not resourceful enough."

Wang was stunned. He would have fallen over from shock if the force field hadn't held him upright. Betrayed again, this time by the woman he loved! "Why?" he asked. "Why . . . you do it?"

She caressed the edge of the force field, and Wang imagined he could feel her hands slide along his skin. Even with this new knowledge, the effect was immediate and painful; the force field held *everything* in place.

"I'm a plant," Flo said.

"You told me that. Why you want . . . destroy world?"

She shook her head. "No, I meant that literally. I'm a plant. Daddy found out how to cross the kingdom barrior as well as the species barrier. I'm half orchid."

"Impossible!" Wang cried, but he knew it wasn't. The way she was always soaking her feet, her love of dirt, her unreasonable fear of fire and smoke, even the color of her skin should have clued him in long ago. He had been blinded by love.

"Why you want to destroy world?" he asked, knowing that *his* world had been destroyed the moment she betrayed him.

She snorted and turned away. "It's all a matter of perspective," she said. "From a plant's point of view, humanity has practically destroyed it already. The Pangaea era was a great time for plants. And for dinosaurs, who never got a fair chance before the asteroid wiped them out. I want to bring that all back and give that world another opportunity to evolve something truly great."

"Dinosaurs?" Wang asked, shocked again. "Why dinosaurs?"

Dr. Exo chuckled throatily, and drew back his hood. The face he revealed was green and scaly, with red eyes set wide apart, a long nose ending in flared nostrils, and sharp teeth rimming a mouth that could have eaten a suckling pig in one bite. "Let's just say it's a family project," he said.

Exo was part dinosaur. And Flo was a plant, in both senses of the word. Wang raged inside the force field, trapped there in shame and frustration. She'd led him astray all along. Except—

"You almost died with me in cave, and again in airplane, and in tanks. Why?"

"We all take risks for what we want." She tilted her head back and laughed. It wasn't quite Exo's maniacal cackle, but it was pretty good. "I wanted *you*. You're the best specimen of humanity there is. When Pangaea is re-formed and plants have taken over the world again, I want you for genetic material. My children will be super-beings. We'll have all the strengths of plants *and* animals. We'll rule the Earth forever."

Wang felt a moment of pride at her words. So she *did* want him. But only for his genes. And he had seen the results of her and Exo's other genetic experiments. He wanted no part in that, not even microscopically.

The thought that his offspring could become twisted beast men like the ones he had fought his way through today infuriated him. It was a violation of everything a man stood for, to take what is fundamentally *him* and twist it into a mockery of its true form.

"This . . . is . . . evil," he said, straining hard against his invisible bonds. "I will . . . stop you."

"Like I said," Exo said, laughing, "this is the same kind of force field that's moving the continents around. Admittedly, I've only tapped into a fraction of it, but more than you can resist. You can't stop anything. It's you that's stopped."

Coldly, mustering the five energies of the void, the wind, fire, water, and earth as he spoke, Wang said, "I am Lo Wang, Shadow Warrior. The darkness . . . made whole . . . the night . . . made flesh. Nothing shall stand in my way!"

He flexed his muscles, concentrating with all his might on resisting the force that gripped his body. Slowly the sword that had been pointing upward came down, inch by painful inch, and Wang moved his right foot forward another inch. His chest felt as if it might burst with the strain, but he tightened his muscles even further and pushed the force field outward.

A loud hum came from the machinery behind Dr. Exo. He turned around, startled. Flo looked from Wang to the machinery, then back to Wang.

"What are you doing?" she demanded, drawing her .38.

"You know ancient Japanese saying," he told her. "Suddenly a Wang shot out."

The edges of her mouth moved upward in just a hint of a smile. Wang knew he had reached her, had touched some inner part of her that actually cared for him. But her smile faded, and she raised her gun to point at his chest.

Wang poured every last bit of energy he could muster into resisting the force field. Even so, his effort wouldn't have mattered if Flo hadn't fired the .38 straight at his heart. But she did, and the shock wave of the bullet hitting the already-stressed force field was all it took to overload the field generator. Sparks flew from the rack of electronics, and the field blew outward with a loud clap of thunder.

The expanding field snatched both Flo and Exo and flung them away like feathers in a tornado. Exo smashed sideways against the metal door, which bent into a perfect impression of his profile before he slumped to the floor, unconscious or dead. Flo bounced off the stone wall and crumpled to the floor beside one of the support columns, which cracked under the sudden wave of force that passed through it.

The massive stone cylinder groaned and shifted sideways, crumbling as it moved. A huge section of it sheared off and fell right beside Flo's head, shaking the entire chamber and spewing rock chips everywhere.

"No!" screamed Wang. Free of the force field now, he rushed toward her, but the rest of the column began to topple before he could get there. He slammed into it with his shoulder and shoved it away from her head, but he couldn't alter its course enough to miss her body completely. With a sickening thud of stone against stone, it crushed her legs and pinned her to the floor.

"Flo!" he cried.

"Wang! Help me!"

He tried. He pushed against the column, trying to roll it off of her legs, but it didn't budge. He hunted frantically for a metal bar he could use as a lever, but there was nothing other than a gun barrel from one of the guards Wang had killed, and that bent like a willow as soon as he put any force behind it. She was trapped.

"Flo, Flo," he said. "We could have been such great team. Lo Wang, Flo Wang—could have been beautiful."

She cried out with the pain, but got it under control and choked out, "It couldn't happen. You would never have accepted my dream."

"I could have given you better one," Wang said sadly.

She tried to say something else, but the pain overwhelmed her and she fainted.

He slumped down beside her, leaning back against the cool stone column. He knew he should leave her there and go look for the ABCD device, but he didn't care anymore. Let the continents smash together. Maybe he would die in the collision. Maybe he and Exo and Flo would go together, and something better than all of them would repopulate the world.

He fingered the nuclear bomb at his waist. He could make sure of it. Yes, why not? What did he have left to live for?

He pulled the bomb out and examined the tiny digital display. It was only a kiloton bomb, hardly big enough to even rattle Ayers Rock, especially with the warren of honeycombed tunnels to absorb the blast, but it would take care of him and Flo and Exo well enough. He set the timer for half an hour. That ought to give the continents time to make their rendezvous. Australia would still be out in mid ocean, but that was fitting. Let it stay separate, a museum of the old species for whatever arrived from the mainland in millennia to come.

He tossed the bomb over his shoulder, heard it bounce down through the tiers of computer consoles. He didn't pay any attention to where it finally came to rest.

A deep growl from directly in front of him got his attention, though. Wang looked up and saw Dr. Exo stagger to his feet. The reptilian creature—a velociraptor-man, Wang guessed—turned toward Wang and bellowed a primal scream of rage. Then he coughed and spoke in English. "Prepare to die," he said.

Chapter 23

Wang shoved himself upright against the stone column, but he had to hold on to it for support. The effort of breaking free from the force field had nearly drained him. Yet here stood his most dangerous adversary yet, for Wang realized that he had never learned a fighting form based on a dinosaur. His teachers had taught him cat forms and dog forms and bird forms—even lizard forms, but no one in all the centuries of martial arts had come up with a velociraptor form.

Wang was completely on his own here. It was skill against skill, mammal against reptile, and the winner would inherit the Earth.

Exo advanced, staggering a bit when he put his weight on his left leg. That was the side that had smashed into the door; Wang bet that entire half of his body hurt. He could use that to his advantage, if he could just stand up long enough to strike.

Ryan Hughes

Now he recognized the unfamiliar smell that had raised the hairs on his neck earlier. It was the smell of dinosaur, instinctive enemy of the creatures that had eventually evolved into Lo Wang. Even now, after all these millennia, it still struck terror into his heart. That was hard-wired into the brain at such a deep level that Wang couldn't override it.

Exo didn't seem to have a similar disadvantage. He laughed softly and said, "You're the pathetic pinnacle of a pathetic race. I am not even the best of my race, but I can easily vanquish you."

Race? Wang thought. Were there more like him, or was Exo merely claiming credit for the past?

It didn't matter. Wang and Exo would both be elementary particles in half an hour. In the meantime, smearing Exo's brains around the room would give Wang something to distract him from the heartache of Flo's treachery.

"Your race was weak," Wang said as he examined his adversary for vulnerable spots. "Gave up when asteroid hit."

"Gave up?" Exo shouted. "The entire world was destroyed!"

"Excuses, excuses," Wang said. He bent down and picked up a fist-sized piece of the stone column that had fallen on Flo. "I have joke for you. What sound does asteroid make when it wipes out dinosaurs?"

Exo squinted his beady red eyes. "Sound?"

"It goes *Wang!*" With the word, he flung the piece of sandstone straight at Exo's head. It hit him square between the eyes with a meaty *thunk* that should have knocked him cold, but Exo merely staggered backward a step, then shook his head and charged.

212

Wang leaped aside, but not fast enough. Exo accelerated in a blur, snarling and snapping at Wang's right arm, sinking his teeth into the same spot where the badger-man had gotten him. Wang hit him in the temple with the edge of his left hand, but Exo's head was hard as rock. Wang needed to hit someplace softer to even get his attention. He lashed out with a foot against Exo's left knee—the side that had hit the door when the force field exploded—and when Exo roared with pain he yanked his arm free. He spun away, kicking out again with three quick strikes at Exo's knee, hip, and side.

"Aarrr!" bellowed the velociraptor-man, shaking the cavern with his voice. But he didn't go down. He whirled around and kicked out backwards at Wang with his good leg. His foot caught Wang in the stomach and knocked the air out of him, then a second kick slammed him up against the back wall of the control room.

Exo tried a third kick, but Wang dodged it. With the wall there he couldn't use Exo's motion against him in a standard karate flip, but he remembered another of Shoji's teachings: For every action, there is an opposite and equal reaction. When Exo hit the wall, the wall pushed back with equal force, and Wang added his own force to it. Bracing himself against the rough stone, he kicked out with both feet at once, catching Exo square in the chest and sending him backward over a smashed computer desk.

Exo crashed through the desk and tipped over another one beyond it, but he rolled to his feet and flung the debris out of his way. He was gasping for breath, but so was Wang. They eyed each other

213

warily while they regained control of their lungs. Wang was drenched in sweat. He knew he was dehydrated from all this heat, but Exo seemed to thrive in it.

Wang reached into a pocket on his belt, took out three shuriken, and flung the first one spinning toward Exo's right eye. Exo jerked his head sideways just as quickly and the shuriken spun past the side of his head. Wang tried again, then sent the third one right after it, hoping Exo would dodge into the last blade. It almost worked, but it was nearly impossible to read the intentions of the unfamiliar velociraptor form. Also, Exo was faster than the human adversaries Wang's reflexes were tuned for; the second shuriken missed completely, and the third one stuck fast in Exo's hard bone forehead.

The point that penetrated bone obviously hadn't gone deep enough to hit brain. Wang glanced down for another rock to drive it deeper with, but that momentary distraction was all Exo needed to launch another attack.

He came at Wang like a New York taxi, straight and belligerent with no intention of turning aside. He lowered his head for the charge. The shuriken in his forehead gleamed in the fluorescent light, a metallic horn on which he clearly intended to impale Wang.

Wang had just been to Spain. He swept his cloak aside and arched backward just as Exo thundered past. "Toro!" he yelled, then he switched to Japanese and shouted again, "Tora, tora, tora!" as he pressed his own attack.

Exo tried to turn around in time to meet him, but Wang kicked him in the side and sent him sprawling into the back wall again, then grabbed his arm before he could recover and flung him toward the open wall into the gallery below.

Exo was too heavy to fly that far, even with all of Wang's leverage behind him. He crashed into his padded leather command chair, snapping it off its dais, and tipped over the control console beyond it. Sparks flew, and Exo howled with pain as he scrambled to his feet again.

Wang needed a weapon, and he needed one *now*. Exo's hide was too tough for karate or even for shuriken. Wang had to find something tougher. A riot gun would be nice, but he had long since run out of ammunition for that. Even a machine gun would be better than nothing, but there were none in evidence except the one Wang had bent trying to save Flo.

Flo! She had a .38. But when Wang looked back at her, still pinned beneath the massive stone column, he saw that she no longer held it in her hand. It had no doubt been flung clear in the force-field explosion. It could be anywhere in the room.

Flo was awake again. Their eyes met, and Wang felt a fresh wave of anguish shiver through him. Betrayed again!

A noise came from the lower gallery. Someone was still alive down there. Wang risked a glance, saw no motion, but a glimmer of silver much closer at hand caught his eye. His sword, flung away by the force field to impale a computer monitor like Excalibur in the stone. With a joyous cry, Wang lunged for it, drew it from the monitor, and pressed the attack.

Exo hissed and started throwing pieces of the destroyed control room at Wang. Computers, their cords trailing like streamers behind them, chairs swiveling like bizarre space stations in orbit; he uprooted entire desks and heaved them at Wang, but Wang either dodged them or cut them in half with his sword and pressed on.

He backed Exo all the way across the control room, but was unable to strike a killing blow. Exo's movements were too unfamiliar; Wang kept misjudging how he would move and where he would dodge. At last the master of evil could back up no more; he was up against the wall with nothing left to throw.

"Hah, you can't evade me forever!" Wang said as he moved in for the kill, but Exo had one more trick up his sleeve. Just as Wang brought down his sword to slice off Exo's head, Exo kicked off from the wall and rolled in mid flight so that his left arm took the blow. Wang's sword sliced completely through it and bit into Exo's side, but the velociraptor-man kept rolling and wrenched the blade from Wang's hands.

"Oh, look, you're coming apart," Wang said, kicking at Exo's hand, which twitched on the floor at his feet.

"A calculated sacrifice," Exo said, pulling the sword from his side with his remaining hand. He spun around and attacked Wang with it—and that was his fatal mistake.

Wang knew sword-fighting. Exo might be part velociraptor, and his body style might be unfamiliar enough to disrupt Wang's deep-seated fighting techniques, but when it came to sword play there were no forms left to discover. Wang had been taught to think of the blade as an entity unto itself, and he had studied every possible motion it could make. Exo held it high and to the right; Wang knew that he would slice down and inward at an angle, and because every action produced an opposite and equal reaction that would unbalance him to that side. It would be even worse with a missing hand, which Exo wouldn't yet realize he needed to compensate for.

Wang lashed out with his foot as the sword came down. Kay equals one half em vee squared, he thought as foot met the flat of the blade at as large a fraction of the speed of light as he could manage. It was a pitifully small fraction, slower even than his own speed of thought, but his kick was fast enough to snap the sword in the middle and send the point flying straight through the leathery skin at Exo's neck. Even at that it had barely been enough; the sword came to rest with six inches or so sticking out in front and only a bloody red point protruding from the back.

Exo gurgled in surprise and dropped the broken sword. Wang snatched it up before it hit the ground and swung it upward to slice off Exo's right hand before he could pull the blade out of his throat.

"Any last words?" Wang asked him, as the other hand twitched next to the first but Exo only gurgled.

"Father!" Flo screamed, her voice echoing in the vast chamber. She couldn't see him from where she lay, but she had heard what Wang said. "Wang, don't kill him!"

He had been about to drive the snapped-off sword into Exo's right eye, but her plea stayed his hand. It didn't matter; Exo opened his mouth and blood gushed out around the sword wound. He staggered to the side, tried to catch himself against a roof support pillar, but the stumps of his arms merely painted the stone red as they brushed past and he fell to his knees. He teetered there for a second, then fell forward, his weight driving the sword point on through his neck when he hit the floor.

"Too late," Wang said softly.

Florelle screamed. Wang waited a moment to make sure Exo was truly dead, then slowly climbed back up to where she lay and knelt down beside the massive pillar.

"You haven't won," she said. "You may have killed us, but the continents can't be reversed. The world of plants and dinosaurs will come again."

Wang opened his mouth to tell her how little he cared, but another voice beat him to it.

"Wrong."

It came from the lower control room. Wang heard a screech of metal on stone as someone dragged a desk across the floor, then Jefferson Adams stuck his round, sweaty face up over the edge.

"Here, give us a hand up," he said.

"Us?" Wang asked.

"I've got Dr. Morgan here with me. Found her topside, waiting for a rescue. You damn near fried her with those two nukes. What were you thinking?"

Nukes. By all the gods, the *nuke!* Wang leaped up and started searching beneath the rubble that he and Exo had made of the upper control room. Where had the nuke gone? Dying in a blaze of subatomic glory

218

was fine when there was nothing left for him to accomplish, but if Dr. Morgan was here then there might still be a chance to prevent the continents from colliding.

"What the hell are you doing?" Adams demanded when he saw Wang digging frantically through the debris. "Help us up here."

"No time!" Wang yelled. "Nuclear bomb here, too!"

"What! Jesus H. Christ, if it isn't one thing it's another." Adams turned to look over his shoulder. "Here, K.D., give me a boost up. Yow, not there!" He squirmed and wiggled and grunted his way up and over the balcony edge, then turned around and pulled up Dr. Morgan.

She was a big woman. Big in all the right places, too. Not slender and graceful like a Japanese woman; she was more the *Playboy* playmate type. That was fine with Wang. He had grown to appreciate the American style of beauty during his time in the States. Even with the threat of nuclear annihilation only minutes away, he paused to take in her charms. Her breasts strained the buttons on her white—but considerably worse for wear—lab coat. Her waist and hips rounded out the perfect hourglass figure. Blond hair shot with a few streaks of early gray framed a face that was round and smooth skinned with sparkling blue eyes and big, full lips. She was flushed red and breathing hard from the heat.

"Nice," Wang said, unaware that he had spoken until she blushed and said, "Likewise, I'm sure." She meant it. Wang recognized that look in her eyes.

"The bomb?" Adams said. "Hello, Earth to Lo Wang. Did you say there was a bomb about to go off?"

Wang dragged his eyes away from Dr. Morgan and looked at the nondescript government man. "Yes. Small bomb, about this big." He held his hands about six inches apart. "Digital display on one side, and—"

"I know what it looks like, for God's sake; I bought it for you, after all. Just before you ran off and left me there without even my credit card to pay the bill with. I had a hell of a time convincing the arms dealer that I wasn't running some kind of stash-and-dash scam." As he spoke, Adams started sifting through the rubble on the floor. "You got any idea where it is, or do we just bumble around until we trip over it?"

"Is near here," Wang said, waving his arms to encompass a space ten or fifteen feet around himself. "I toss it over shoulder, so not see where it go."

"Yep," Adams said, sighing. "This is definitely one of those days. I chase your sorry ass all the way to Australia, get shot down as soon as we get here, parachute out right into a brush fire, damn near get run over by some idiot in a tank, get knocked out by not just one but *two* nuclear blasts, then I find Katie up on top of the Rock and we fight our way through demons from hell to help you out down here, only to find that you've set another bomb you can't find. Boy, oh boy, is it ever going to be Miller time when I get home."

"Here it is." Dr. Morgan bent over—a motion that Wang watched with rising interest—and extracted the bomb from where it had wedged beside a smashed workbench. She examined it for a moment, then pushed a button.

"Don't!" Adams shouted, but she ignored him and pressed two or three more.

"There," she said, tossing the black metal oblong to him. "Defused. Now let's see about the ABCD device, shall we?"

Chapter 24

Adams took the bomb in his hands. He looked over at Wang, and Wang could tell just what he was thinking.

"It would take fifty of you," Wang told him, "and bomb would still wind up in *your* ass." He walked past Adams and held out his arm for Dr. Morgan, then led her upward through the debris to the electronics racks at the back of the room.

"My, you certainly made a mess of things, didn't you?" she asked, stepping up to a phone-booth-sized rack of equipment with a big red slot-machine-style handle on the side. Actually, it had survived the fight mostly intact. Green and red lights still glowed above switches and dials, meters still jiggled left and right, and a low humming sound still issued from the massive transformers at the base of it. But one bank of equipment was dark, and that was what Dr. Morgan zeroed in on.

"Tsk, tsk," she said, craning her head around to

look at the back of it. "You've broken the bogon particle stream inverter. I'm surprised it didn't blow up completely when you—wait a minute. Somebody's tapped into it." She traced the wires over to the rack of equipment beside the door.

"It looks like a force field generator," she said.

"Yes," Wang told her. "Wang trapped. Had to push very hard. Make big bang when break free."

"Destroying the add-on field generator instead of the bogon inverter. I see." She looked at him with undisguised lust. "My, but you must be strong to do that."

Wang grinned like a schoolboy and looked away before he could blush. His gaze fell on Flo, still pinned under the column, and he lost his grin. He hadn't been strong enough to save her.

Dr. Morgan moved back to the first rack of equipment and began rearranging wires. She pushed a few buttons and the dead component came to life, then she grabbed the large red handle on the side and said, "Hang on to your jockstraps, boys. The Earth's about to move."

She pulled the lever. Wang felt the same kind of momentary disorientation that he'd felt when he'd keyed in the wrong value for the Earth's rotation. Nothing else happened for a minute, and he began to relax, but then the vibration in the floor that he'd grown used to grew suddenly worse. A wave traveled through the cavern, tilting them sideways, then back upright again. A moment later the ground jolted upward, hard.

Rock groaned under the strain. Wang imagined the entire mile-and-a-half-by-mile-wide-by-thousand-foot-high mass of Ayers Rock dropping down through the layers of catacombs that Exo had tunneled beneath it, squashing them all like bugs under a heel, but the support pillars held the ceiling in place. A little dust showered down, but that was all.

Not for Flo. She screamed, and Wang ran across the control room to her side. The pillar that had pinned her by the legs had rolled in the quake; it now straddled her body just below the hips.

"You've ruined everything!" she cried.

"We've saved the world," Dr. Morgan said. She walked over beside Wang and said, "I've reversed the motion of the continents, only much slower. They'll move back into place over the next couple of weeks."

"Damn you!" Flo said. "Damn you all."

"Who's she?" Dr. Morgan asked Wang.

Adams had come behind her. "What do you mean? Don't you recognize your own daughter?"

Dr. Morgan narrowed her eyes at him. "Her? I've never seen this woman before in my life."

"She told me she was your daughter," Adams said. "Begged to go along with Wang to rescue you."

"She is plant," Wang said. "Orchid-woman, and spy. Moving continents was her idea."

"It was a brilliant plan," Flo said, struggling for the breath to form words. "With humanity out of the way, my father and I would have created a far better world than this sorry arrangement."

"That's a matter of opinion," said Adams, but he was rubbing his chin in a thoughtful manner.

Flo seemed to wilt a little. "Hang on," Wang told her. "I get this off you somehow."

She didn't answer at first, and when she did, her

voice was only a whisper. "For what?" she asked. "To spend the rest of my life in jail?" She dropped her head to her arms.

"Flo!" Wang said. He touched her cool, smooth cheek with his fingertips, slid them down to her neck to feel for a pulse, but found none.

"She's dead," said Adams. "And not a moment too—"

Wang reached out and snapped the little finger on Adams's left hand before the man could even flinch.

"Ow-wwww!" Adams curled around his hand and slumped to the floor. Beside him, Flo lay in silence, as dignified in death as she had been when she was in a hundred times his pain.

Dr. Morgan pulled Wang away from both of them. "Come on," she said. "We're done here. Let's get out of this place. It's hot as hell, and it gives me the creeps."

"One last thing," said Wang. "Then we go." He crouched down beside Adams. "Name, please."

"Huh?"

"Name. Tanaka's first name. Man who will lead me to Zilla."

Adam looked at him incredulously. "My God, after all this, you still want to go after Zilla? Why?"

"Matter of honor," Wang said. "You wouldn't understand. Now give me name." He reached for Adams's hand again.

"Takeshi," Adams said quickly. "The guy's name is Takeshi."

Wang frowned. "Takeshi Tanaka," he said.

"That's right."

"That is probably most common name in all Japan.

You know how many Takeshi Tanakas there are in world?"

Adams puffed out his chest. "Yes, as a matter of fact, I do. Assuming none of them were killed in the earthquakes, of course, there are six million, four hundred and seventy thousand, eight hundred and ten. Happy hunting."

Wang considered killing him for his insolence, but the sight of Flo lying there beside him stayed his hand. He wouldn't profane her resting place with Adams's blood. And in truth, Adams had kept his part of the bargain. Assuming, of course, that one of the millions of Takeshi Tanakas in the world could really lead Wang to Zilla, but he had no doubt that one of them could. With that many of them out there, it would be incredible if one of them *couldn't*.

He felt a giggle rise to the surface. By the time it reached his throat, it was a full-blown laugh. Wang threw back his head and made the cavern echo with his mirth.

Adams grinned. "I'm glad you see the funny side of it."

Wang let his laughter wind down, then said, "Ancient Japanese saying: Laugh or cry, live or die, all same to gods."

"Look at the bright side. You saved the world. Zilla's still out there somewhere. You've got plenty of time to seek out your revenge if that's what you want to do."

Wang stood up and took Dr. Morgan's hand. "I kill you another day, Mr. *Adams*. Tell Zilla I kill him another day as well." He tilted his head, struck by a sudden thought, then said, "Probably on a Saturday.

Yes, I think I make it a Saturday. That is Doyobi, Earth-day in Japan. Very appropriate, you agree?"

"Very, but I don't know Zilla," Adams said.

"Nine more fingers say you do," Wang said. "Don't push luck." He turned away with Dr. Morgan and walked to the door. Exo's impression in the metal had captured an eternal moment of surprised agony; Wang smiled as he wrenched the door open and held it while Dr. Morgan stepped through.

He looked back at Adams, then over to Florelle. Both silent figures were already part of his past. Adams might become part of his future as well. It was a gamble, but one worth taking. Wang might not be able to find Zilla directly, but he would always be able to find Adams. And eventually, if Wang bided his time, Adams would lead him to the man he really wanted. In the meantime, Saturdays would be very bad days for the master of evil.

Epilogue

The office building was less than a mile from the shipyard in Los Angeles where Wang had first come to America. Of course the shipyard, once it was rebuilt, would be considerably closer due to the tidal waves and the lowering of the California Crustal Plate, but that was a minor detail in a reshaped world.

The gigantic penthouse office at the top of the building had weathered the earthquakes without damage. It had the aura of a place that might outlast the Earth itself. It smelled of jasmine and other, more exotic scents. The evening light barely penetrated the curtains that were drawn to within an inch of one another across the ten-foot-high windows. In the middle of the back wall, shrouded in shadows, stood a huge ebony desk. Behind that desk sat a figure in a hooded cloak.

The man who had been Jefferson Adams, and who would call himself Grant Carter when he left the office, stood before the desk, trying not to look like he was interested in seeing into the shadows.

"You misplaced Cuba," the gravelly voice of his employer said. There was a degree of amusement in the voice, as well as a threat. Cuba had been a good source of cheap labor.

"Vanished in the Bermuda Triangle," Adams said, shrugging his shoulders in a beats-me gesture.

"And Iraq? I suppose the clockwise rotation of Saudi Arabia was just another mysterious accident?"

Adams smiled. "Africa was in the way. What could we do?"

A low chuckle. A dragon purring might make such a sound. "I suppose you are to be commended, considering the difficulty of the task set before you. The world is substantially the same as it was, perhaps even improved. At any rate, my interests have been protected from that upstart Exo's foolish plans. You have my thanks."

"Just doing my job."

"Of course." The shadowy figure leaned forward. "And Lo Wang? What of him? You did not kill him."

Adams rubbed his splinted and bandaged little finger. "That would have been beyond my capabilities."

"At least you are honest." Leather squeaked as the figure leaned back in his chair again. "Do not trouble yourself with Lo Wang. His day will come soon enough."

"I'm sure it will," said Adams. He swallowed nervously, then said, "Speaking of days, he gave me a message for Zilla."

"I will pass it along," said the gravelly voice.

Adams didn't let even a quiver of his lip betray the smile he was feeling. Wang's words would go no further than this room, he was sure. They wouldn't need to. But he was glad to keep up the pretense if Zilla wanted to.

"Wang said he would kill Zilla on a Saturday."

There was a long silence, then, "That was all?"

"Yes."

"You may go."

Adams nodded and turned away. He walked the thirty paces to the door in silence, opened it, stepped through, and closed it softly behind him.

The shadowy figure waited until he heard the latch click before he reached out with an unsteady hand for his desk calendar. He paused a few inches short of it, then withdrew his hand. He really didn't want to know.